DETOURS

A Novel about the Resiliency of the Human Spirit

Carol Fricke

Joshua Tree
Publishing

• Chicago •

DETOURS
A Novel about the Resiliency of the Human Spirit

CAROL FRICKE

Published by

Joshua Tree Publishing
JoshuaTreePublishing.com
• Chicago •

13-Digit ISBN Trade Paper: 978-1-956823-41-7
13-Digit ISBN Hard Cover: 978-1-956823-46-2
13-Digit ISBN eBook: 978-1-956823-48-6

Disclaimer:
This is a work of fiction. Names, characters, places, and incidents are the product of the author's imagination or have been used fictitiously. Any resemblance to actual persons, living or dead, events, locales or organizations is entirely coincidental.

Printed in the United States of America

DEDICATION

To Al

My husband

My love story

And to

The Susquehanna Service Dogs

Who change lives every day

PROLOGUE

Everybody has a story. I think about this as I watch the dogs frolic in the cool night air. I like hearing people's stories. The twists and turns, the decisions—or lack of them—that bring them to where they are now. And fate, luck, divine intervention, or whatever you want to call it that plays a part in their journey.

I'm not one to talk about myself. I have always preferred the comfort of listening. But as I watch Jed, his black coat blending into the darkness, his head lifted to the night sky, smelling the air, I realize I have a story to tell, and so does he.

CHAPTER 1

HALEY DUNCAN

It is another Saturday of keeping myself busy. Looking out my car window, I see life moving by me at a fast pace. Women with shopping bags, men in suits, teens with backpacks, all in a hurry, all with a purpose. Not too long ago, that used to be me. However, that was before. Now is after. I'm not exactly sure when I started measuring my life in terms of "before" and "after," but I know it's been within the last two years. Shaking my head, I turn up the music in hopes that it will lighten my mood.

"I hate traffic," I mutter to myself.

Being around all this action and noise hurts me in a sad way and accentuates the loneliness I feel. It reminds me of what a masquerade my life has become. For the last two years, I've lived my life with my "game face" on. No one has been invited to see below the surface where I keep the pain hidden. Even though I have people who love and care about me, our lives are so different that I don't feel they'll understand. If this were a movie instead of my real life, I could win an Academy Award for the acting I've been doing.

I am relieved when I finally pull into the parking lot of the Homeland Service Dog Association. Volunteering here has been my refuge for the past two years. Getting out of the car, I can feel my mood lighten as I walk up the lane and open the door. Today I'll be spending time with puppies, and that is just what I need.

Cody Hayes, one of the trainers, looks up from his phone. "Hey, Haley, good to see you. Do you have those hugging arms ready?"

"Always," I say with a smile.

"Well, have fun. You know how important this job is," he replies.

"I do. I'm their new adventure for the day," I answer.

I feel him watching me as I sit down on the floor in the enclosure, but I don't hear the door close when he leaves. My whole focus is on the seven fuzz balls of Labrador retriever puppies surrounding me. Almost immediately, I have two inquisitive little guys crawling over my legs. I pick up the closest one and cradle him in my arms. I breathe in his smell and gently pet his soft baby hair. Memories flood back to me of the first dog that Jack and I raised together. We were in total agreement about our priorities—get married, buy a house, start with a dog, then the kids.

We had no idea what we were doing when we brought Dewey home, our first Golden retriever puppy. Our house still had that new-house smell when I carried him through the front door for the first time. Jack headed upstairs to change as I put Dewey down so I could hang up my coat. When I turned back around, Dewey was making himself right at home by pooping on the new carpet. Yelling for Jack, I picked him up mid-poop and headed for the door. Thinking that disaster had struck, Jack came running down the stairs in his bare feet and stepped right into the newly laid pile. That's how the three of us initiated our new house and carpet.

Even now that Jack and Dewey are no longer with me, the memory cuts through the pain of their loss and can still make me smile. Through the years, this became our favorite dog story, and Jack and I used to enjoy helping each other tell it to our friends and acquaintances.

"How's it going?" Cody asks as he returns to the room, interrupting my reminiscing.

"Good. How else could it be with seven puppies vying for my attention?" I respond.

"Remember, what you're doing is important. Early socialization is one of the most valuable experiences we can give these puppies," he says.

"I know. Jack and I raised three dogs."

Looking up at Cody, I can see his discomfort, and right away, I regret what I said. My guess is that he hasn't lived through his first tragedy yet, being in his early twenties.

"It's OK. It's been two years now," I say, trying to move past the mention of my late husband.

"Do you still miss him?" Cody asks.

"Every day," I reply.

"I can't imagine what that must have been like for you," he says.

"Nobody can," I respond honestly. Realizing that was pretty much a conversation stopper, I give my full attention back to the puppies, and Cody gives his full attention back to his phone. The puppies continue climbing in and out of my arms. One has fallen asleep on my legs, and another one is fascinated with my shoelaces. Before I know it, my hour of puppy hugging is over. As I leave the enclosure, Cody looks up and asks, "Could you see yourself taking one of these guys home?"

"If I were you, I would be sure to count them before I go," I say as I bend over and pet the one little guy who followed me to the gate.

"I've been watching you around the dogs. You're good. We need more volunteers like you. Have you ever considered raising one of these guys for us?" he asks.

"Oh, I couldn't. It would be too hard for me to give him up," I quickly reply.

"That's what they all say at first, but we have eighty-five puppy raisers right now."

"Eighty-five! Where did you find that many people willing to raise and train a puppy for a year and a half and then give it up?" I ask.

"They come from all over, and they pretty much can be anybody. We have couples, families, single people, senior citizens, and college students raising puppies for us right now. But we are always on the lookout for new raisers. We never have enough. I'm on my third puppy," he says.

"You've done it three times!"

"Yep. Most of our raisers don't stop after one dog. I couldn't be prouder of my three, even the first one who didn't make it through the program."

"What happened?"

"We found hip issues. Right now, he's probably lying in front of my window, waiting for me to come home."

"You got to keep him?" I ask.

"I didn't have to, but I figured Leroy, my shepherd, needed a buddy," Cody says.

"Dogs need a dog friend. We learned that after Dewey, our first dog. I have two at home right now."

"I think you would be a good puppy raiser. You've already learned most of our training methods through your volunteering."

"I don't . . ."

"Listen, you're a teacher, right?"

"Yes."

"Do you like what you do?"

"I love what I do."

"Well, don't you get attached to your students every year?"

"Sure, but . . ."

"But you let them go. You teach them and then send them out into the world to make a difference."

"I really don't think that is a fair comparison."

"I think it is. Look, for whatever it's worth. I bet you're a great teacher. I know you're a great volunteer, and I bet you would be a great puppy raiser. You're stronger than you think. Plus, you have two dogs at home that can help you."

"It's an act. Some days I'm barely hanging on, but thank you for the kind words."

"Promise me you'll think about it," he says.

Looking at Cody, I see the earnestness of youth. I see this in my students too. I miss this in myself.

"I'll add it to my list of thoughts," I reply as I give him a smile, knowing full well that I just told him a little white lie. As I leave the kennel and walk out to my car, I wish I were back with the puppies. It was the first time in a long time that I felt happy.

CHAPTER 2

MARK LANCER

O n a beautiful evening like this, I would probably have been out mowing the lawn. That was before I started living in a condo, where professionals handle these jobs. Now, my options are limited to either staring at the television or taking a walk around the block. I choose the walk.

As I start my journey around the neighborhood, I can't help thinking about how I ended up here. My life certainly hasn't gone according to plan. But then again, I wonder how many people's lives really do. Things were fine—not great, but fine until three years ago. Then all hell broke loose. I've heard that life events happen in threes, and that is exactly how it unfolded for me. Within five months, my son left for college, Melissa filed for divorce, and the accident happened. All were life-changing, but of the three, my accident had the most devastating effects.

It's been three long years since it happened, and there's still no cure in sight. I wonder how many more years it will take before I'm back to normal. That is if I ever get back to normal. I keep telling myself that I should be thankful for what I have instead of what I've lost. But that's a lot easier said than done. I feel like my body has betrayed me and I'm damaged goods. This I won't tell my doctors or anyone else. I was never a big talker before the accident, and I'm definitely not one now. Even though I keep tight control of all my anger and frustrations, they continue to eat away at me. I wish my gloom would fade with each step I take, but it never does. I can usually push these thoughts aside during the course of my workday, but there is something about walking alone that brings them front and center.

"Nice lawn," I say as I walk by a man trimming around his mailbox.

"Thanks. All this rain helps," he replies.

I wish I could trade places with him. Even though I don't know the slightest thing about him, his life has to be better than mine. I miss taking care of something or someone. I'm tired of being alone and having everything centered around me. Even now, in the back of my mind, I keep thinking my doctors would frown at this walk I'm taking, but I justify it to myself by checking out all the activity that is going on around me. If I have a seizure here and now, someone is bound to notice.

My accident was just that—an accident. I have to quit making it personal. I was unlucky enough to be in the wrong place at the wrong time. I often play out the "what ifs" in my mind. What if I had been at my normal stakeout spot? What if I hadn't stopped that particular car? What if they didn't pull over right next to the guardrail? It's been three years, and I'm still stuck in the "what ifs." The counselor that the doctors made me see kept preaching acceptance. That's easy for him to say. He didn't have to worry about having a seizure in the middle of our session. I finally convinced him that I was doing fine and moving on, so now I don't have to see him anymore. Those sessions were torture for me.

I know I should be more thankful for what Sergeant Dean did for me. He could have easily thanked me for my service and put me on disability. That I couldn't have handled. My life would lack any type of purpose, and I would have no reason to get up in the morning. Instead, he delegated me to a desk job and some instructing at the station and academy. At least I am still doing some type of police work.

Not being medically cleared to drive is a real pain. Greg, my best friend and fellow trooper, has told me time after time, "I'm only a phone call away. All you have to do is ask, and I will gladly give you a lift."

But I don't ask. I refuse to be a bother or a burden. I really just want to be left alone. Although I absolutely hate not being able to drive, I see it in my mind as only a temporary inconvenience. I got what I consider to be my worst blow on my first day back at work.

"Mark, I hate to do this, but you have to surrender your piece. The doctors won't clear you to carry," said Sergeant Dean.

"You're taking away my gun?" I stammered, totally caught off guard by this.

"Hopefully, this is temporary," he replied.

Like everything else so far, temporary has lasted three years now. I am a cop without a gun, and this continues to be a real sore issue for me.

As I turn the corner and enter a small community park, I find myself surrounded by all the different colors of green. In a few months, most of these greens will change to reds, yellows, and browns. I like experiencing the four seasons, and I hope this won't have to change for me. I have lived my whole life in Pennsylvania, and I can't imagine this not being my home. As I take in my surroundings, I notice two women walking about fifty feet ahead of me on the trail. From the back, the one on the left reminds me of my ex-wife. Those are not pleasant thoughts, even after all this time.

Since the divorce, I've had a lot of time to analyze my marriage, and I've figured out a few things. If I had dated more women, I probably would have recognized how ill-suited Melissa and I were for each other. When I met her in college, it was hard to get past her sex appeal. She was a knockout then, and reluctantly, I have to admit that she is still a beautiful woman today. At school, I was shy and inexperienced, so I admired her from a distance, thinking she was totally out of my league. But for some reason, which I never understood, she picked me over all the other guys vying for her attention. I fell in love hard and for the first time in my life. I remember thinking how great life would be with her by my side. Everything happened fast, and we got married soon after graduation.

Looking back, I am sure she visualized a different kind of life for herself. She was upset when I chose the Pennsylvania State Police Academy over the FBI. She never understood or accepted my choice. I don't think she ever planned on being a policeman's wife. She refused to attend any of our social functions and showed no interest in being friends with any of the other wives. She never did adjust to the rotating shift schedule of a state trooper and complained about it bitterly for most of our married life. She became pregnant with MJ by my first placement, and he filled up her days. For some reason, it seemed like all her love was for him, and she didn't have enough left for me. As time went on, her complaints intensified, and I was always at fault. I never earned enough or did enough to make her happy. I always felt that someday we would find common ground again and be able to get our marriage back on track. But looking back, I can see that she was just biding her time. We dropped MJ off at college on a Saturday, and she was gone on Monday. She never looked back. I wish I could say the same.

MJ is the only bright spot in my life. He keeps me from giving up on myself. Even though he's away at college, I still feel his presence with me every day. It was his idea that I apply for a service dog. After meeting one at school, he became insistent that I apply. I'm not crazy about the idea. It's not the dog part that bothers me. I've always liked dogs, and although I never had a police dog, I greatly admire the work they do. The last time I lived with a dog was when I was a kid. Bear, a mixture of who-knows-what, was my constant companion growing up. If it were my choice, I would have liked MJ to grow up with a dog. I have always felt that animals can provide a wealth of life lessons for growing children. Bear sure did for me. But Melissa was not an animal lover, so to MJ's disappointment and mine, I didn't push the issue. So owning a dog is not the reason why I've been reluctant to apply. I realize having a service dog can be a safety net for me. What I'm having trouble winding my head around is the fact that I'll be advertising to the world that I'm disabled. I'm not sure my ego can handle that. To quiet MJ, I did fill out the preliminary application online. I'm still not sold on the idea, but it made him happy. I guess it doesn't hurt to investigate all my options.

As I round the corner, I see my condo up ahead. After all this time, I still remind myself that this is home. I have to admit it's a nice enough place. Everything is on one floor, and that suits my needs. I am flanked on the right by an eighty-seven-year-old woman and on the left by a couple in their seventies. At forty-five years old, I never dreamed I would be living this type of life. As I get my keys out of my pocket, I look down the row of homes. I still can't picture my future here.

CHAPTER 3

HALEY DUNCAN

The second year is worse than the first. This I didn't expect. Surfing through the channels, I try to find something to occupy my mind and fill the emptiness. How is it that we have all these channels, yet I can't seem to find anything worth watching? Tossing the remote, I remind myself that there is no "we" anymore. I move down to the floor beside Magic, and he plops his head on my lap. Thinking back on the day, I can almost feel those puppies crawling all over me again.

Cody's idea was crazy. "Me, a puppy raiser," I say to Magic. "Right. That's just what I need, something else to break my heart."

I glance at the clock and discover it is later than I like to stay up on a school night. Magic watches me as I let her head drop out of my lap and stand up. She and Thunder, who has been keeping his eye on me from across the room, immediately get up.

As I walk through the house, turning off lights and making sure all the doors are locked, I think about this second year. My teaching has been my salvation. During the day, school occupies so much of my thoughts and takes up so much of my efforts. At home, I have Magic and Thunder to keep me company, so I am not alone.

It is those moments that school and my dogs don't fill that are the hardest for me. The nights are the worst. Falling asleep does not come easily anymore. This is the time when I feel the loneliest and most vulnerable.

After tossing and turning for what seems like hours, I push the covers aside and get out of bed. I quickly search for the dogs to make sure they don't pose any roadblocks as I get up. Opening the sliding glass door, I take refuge on the back deck, where I am surrounded by the night. Here I can feel Jack's presence more than I can at any time during the daylight hours. It surprises me that my most vivid and favorite memories of Jack are not what I expect.

Although the engagement, wedding, anniversaries, and trips were all wonderful, it is the small moments that I replay in my mind. I can still see Jack with my father, both in total concentration, working together on a crossword puzzle during the visit before he died. I can still hear my laughter that time at the shore when he dropped his ice cream all over himself. I remember vividly the day he held me in his arms as we both cried over the death of our first dog. These are the types of moments I remember and cherish the most. Looking up to the stars, I wonder what he would remember.

After all this time, I'm still surprised this happened to Jack. Going in, we both had little experience with death. I guess we were under the misguided reality that our grandparents would die first, then our parents, then us. Death was something reserved for old people or unhealthy people, but not someone like Jack. How naive we were to consider ourselves special or immune.

It doesn't seem fair that only a few words can change your whole existence. When Jack started to feel sick, he was only forty-one. We never suspected that something could be really wrong. We started with our family doctor, who referred him to a specialist, who then referred him to another expert. That's when we began to believe that this could be bad. For us, the fear of not knowing was just about as bad as the fear of knowing. It was almost a relief when he was ultimately diagnosed with pancreatic cancer. Then we knew the battle he was facing, and the treatments could finally begin.

In a rare moment of sharing, he said to me, "I'm not worried about you, Haley. You have enough strength for both of us. 'Defeat' is not a word in your vocabulary. You will be consulting with the doctors for the next treatment when I'm taking my dying breath."

How I wish I hadn't stopped him. It would be easier on me now if we had talked about his impending death. Since his medical options were not depleted, I felt we still had time. I hate myself for not reminding him how much he meant to me. He was the best decision I ever made.

The end came so suddenly. I woke one morning, and as I was drifting in and out of sleep, I remember thinking how quiet and peaceful Jack was. As I rolled over to wish him good morning, I found him unresponsive. I was shocked and unprepared to discover that he had died during the night. I always thought that when someone dies, it would be a dramatic moment, like in the movies. But for us, it's like he stole away quietly into the night. We never got to say goodbye. I wish words of love and a reminder that my heart will never forget him could have been the last words he ever heard.

The first year after Jack died was still filled with Jack. After the funeral, I took five different trips to spread his ashes in the places he loved. His hometown, the shore, his favorite fishing hole, our engagement spot, and his father's grave were all places that were important to him. Each stop was like its own little memorial service for me, bringing back memories of that time in his life.

It took me months to write the thank-you cards to everyone who was so wonderful during his illness. I know I could have mass emailed my thanks, but that didn't feel right for the outpouring of support I received. As an English teacher, writing is what I do and a part of who I am. Those notes filled up many empty hours, helped me work through my emotions, and let me reminisce about Jack.

After his death, I found friends and family were still supportive, but there was an awkwardness to it. They would ask me how I was doing, but I could see they were relieved when I gave them short answers. "I'm doing OK" or "I'm lonely, but I'm fine" was all most people wanted to hear. I realize that my friends and relatives are grieving too, and maybe that's why they don't know what to say to me. Lynn, a fellow teacher and my best friend at school, said it best.

"Haley, I couldn't get Jack out of my mind last night. I cooked beef tenderloin, and I remembered how much he loved that meal when I had you two over for dinner. Jack is such a big part of so many good memories for us. We both miss him terribly."

I couldn't resist giving her a hug. "Thanks, please don't stop remembering him and telling me about it. It's nice to know he's not forgotten."

By the second year, everyone expects you to have settled in and moved on. Now, instead of telling me not to make any drastic changes, everyone is encouraging me to do just that. Family and friends are all asking me the same question: "Are you planning on staying in that big house all by yourself?" I just heard this question yesterday from Steve, my next-door neighbor who is my go-to guy for house and yard questions.

"Have you thought of selling the house and moving into a condo?" he asked.

"No! I love this house. Jack and I finally got it the way we wanted it. With the big fenced yard out back and the dog doors, where else could the dogs and I be so comfortable?" I didn't add that all my memories are here and that I can still feel Jack's presence in the house with me.

"I know how important those dogs are to you. Remember, don't be shy about asking for help. We are right next door," he reminded me.

"I know. I couldn't ask for better neighbors than you and Faith," I replied, and I meant that. Jack and I always felt lucky to have such wonderful and caring neighbors.

The tragedy of my infertility taught me about grieving. Many of the emotions I experienced with that are the same that I feel now. Jack and I struggled to conceive for many years, and I continue to struggle being childless in a world full of children. I would have loved to raise a child we created. It would bring me such comfort to have a living part of Jack still with me. I will never forget his words to me when I was reeling from another month of useless attempts.

"It's going to be OK. This is a tragedy that we're going to work our way through together. But as much as I want a child, you need to know this. You will always be enough for me."

My infertility and Jack's death . . . I never could have imagined my life would take such detours. I'm trying to move on, but healing is such a slow process.

The night air is beginning to chill me, so I leave the haven of the deck and return to the bedroom. It is the wee hours of the morning, and surprisingly, I feel wide awake. I look at Thunder, curled up on Jack's side of the bed. He lifts his head and looks at me with those all-knowing brown eyes. I whisper to him, "I know. You miss him too."

CHAPTER 4

MARK LANCER

It's been a long time since I've watched the snow-laden trees pass by my car window mile after mile. I glance over at MJ as he searches for another radio station. With one hand on the steering wheel and body relaxed back into the seat, he is the essence of youth.

"It's good to get my car running again," I say.

"Yours is a lot more fun to drive than mine," he replies.

"I thought mine would be more comfortable for the road trip."

"You got that right." He chuckles. "I'm really surprised it started right up after all the sitting it has been doing."

"Me too," I say. But I can't help but add, "You shouldn't be doing this for me. Your Christmas break is short already. I'm taking you away from your friends."

"Dad, we've been over this already. Remember, this was my idea in the first place. I'm glad the timing worked out perfectly for me to accompany you. This way, I make sure you get there and don't back out," he adds with a grin. "Are you nervous?" he asks.

"No, 'curious' is more like it," I respond.

"Do you know what they will ask?"

"No, but I've been through plenty of interviews. Usually, I was the one on the giving end."

"What swayed you to apply?" MJ asks, looking over at me.

"You did. You can be pretty convincing. Are you sure you don't want to be a lawyer instead of a doctor?"

"Good one, Dad."

"Anyway, it was an idea worth looking into."

"I'm glad you decided to do this."

"Well, nothing's done yet."

"But wouldn't it be nice if a dog could alert you to an upcoming seizure?"

"I find it hard to believe that an animal can do that."

"They say dogs are very perceptive. The least it can do is cushion your fall and find your cell phone."

"How do you know all this?"

"Remember the girl at school with the dog? Lucky was the dog's name, and he was amazing. That was the first time I ever learned about seizure-alert dogs. Did you hear about them before I started hassling you to get one?"

"I think I read about them in some of the literature my doctor gave me."

"Did you ever see yourself doing this?"

"No. I still look at my seizures as being temporary."

"Dad, it's been three years."

"Three long years," I say.

"That's exactly why you need to do this now. Maybe you'll be lucky, and when your name comes up on the service dog list, you might not need one. But then again, you might."

"Hey, a little optimism here would be nice."

"You know I'm always rooting for you. I know this is a good idea."

"I appreciate your concern, MJ."

"Sarah told me how Lucky changed her life. A dog could change yours, too, for the better."

"We'll see."

I look over at MJ, waiting. I've had the feeling all break that he wanted to talk to me about something. I kept thinking it was the service dog, but I'm not so sure it isn't something else. Maybe it's a girl, or maybe it's some kind of trouble.

"Is there something else you want to talk to me about, MJ? I've had this feeling all Christmas that there's something you want to say to me. Am I right?"

"It's the cop in you, Dad. You were always perceptive. I was never able to hide anything from you. Not that I had much to hide."

"Out with it."

"I've been offered a great opportunity to study in Spain for my last semester of college. Other than the plane fare, it's not going to cost any more money. I need to do this to improve my Spanish. You know how I want to be bilingual, and I'm running out of time before I start med school."

I quickly mask the surprise and doubt in my eyes. "You sure you have to go all the way to Spain to improve your Spanish?" I say. "Does this have anything to do with a girl?"

"Yes to the first and no to the second."

I wait. I'm stalling for time, trying to figure out how to respond. Finally, I say, "Well, there is time to decide. It's not until next year."

"No, there isn't time. I'm sorry I put off telling you about it. I knew this would be hard for you. I've already filled out all the paperwork and have been accepted. They are just waiting for a yes or no."

"And a deposit, I'm sure," I say.

"And a deposit."

"You know, with these seizures, I don't like to fly."

"I know, Dad."

I can feel the loneliness already. "I will miss you, you know."

"I will miss you too, Dad."

"I suppose your mother is on board with this?"

"You know Mom. It gives her a good excuse to travel."

"Promise me at least a month-long visit this summer."

"Promise."

"I'm going to hold you to that."

"I have already made it a part of my plans," he says. "We Lancer men keep our promises."

"That is something Grandpa used to say," I respond.

"I heard it from you, Dad."

He looks over at me, and in that quick glance, I can see all the things he really wants to say to me. I hope he knows I feel the same.

A couple of miles go by in silence. "It's been nice having you around for more than a few days," I say.

"It's been great, Dad, and I promise I'll come for a month this summer. In the future, if you get a service dog, you won't be so alone. The two of you can take care of each other."

"We'll see" is all I can say.

The remainder of the time passes quickly. The address is outside the town of Homeland and down a long lane. It makes sense that there are no neighbors in sight. Hearing some barking, I guess the kennel is the large building to my right. The offices where my appointment is must be the smaller building to my left.

"What are you going to do with yourself during my interview?" I ask.

"I just thought I would drive around the town and take in the sights until you're done," MJ says.

"I don't know how long it will take."

"No problem for me. Text me when you're done."

A small, elderly lady greets me at the door. "Mr. Lancer, come on in. You're right on time. Follow me."

I take a seat in what appears to be a small meeting room. I don't wait for more than five minutes when the door opens.

"Mr. Lancer, I'm Cody Hayes, one of the trainers here at the Homeland Service Dog Association. This is Alfie Grey, another one of our trainers, and this is Timber, one of our dogs in advanced training."

After shaking hands with the trainers, I bend down to greet the small yellow Lab. "Timber, what a great name for a beauty like you."

"She's a great dog. We haven't matched her yet, but we have a number of possibilities."

Cody motions for me to sit down, and they take the two seats facing me. "Tell Timber to visit," he says to me.

"Visit?" I say, somewhat confused.

Timber comes over to me and rests her head on my knee.

"Oh, I get it." I pet her head, feeling the silkiness of her hair.

"Pat your thighs," Cody says.

I do so, and Timber puts her front paws and the upper part of her body on my lap. I ruffle her ears and slide my hands up and down her body. "This is nice."

Cody lets her remain there for a minute and then says, "Off," and Timber returns to the floor. When he says, "Come," she stands in front of him. He takes his keys out of his pocket and throws them on the floor. "Take it," he says. Timber walks over to the keys, picks them up in her mouth, and looks at Cody. "Hold," he instructs. She waits there, looking at him. At "Give," she walks over and drops the keys in Cody's hand. "Down," he says next, and Timber lies down on the floor, rolling onto one hip. "Stay."

"That's impressive," I say.

"All our dogs know certain basic commands. Once they are matched with a client, we train them specifically for that person's needs."

"Like my seizures."

"Like your seizures," Cody says. "Now, Mr. Lancer—"

I interrupt, "Mark."

"OK, Mark. We see from your application that you are a state policeman."

"Yes."

"Why did you choose that line of work?" Alfie, the other trainer, asks.

"I came from a law enforcement family. I knew when I was very young that I wanted to be a cop. That is all I ever wanted to be."

"Why did you choose the state police?" Alfie asks.

"I almost joined the FBI, but I thought the state police suited me better. I liked everything about the job except the paperwork."

"What's the best part of the job?" she asks.

"I like helping people, and the job forces you to be at your best at all times. I also like being on the good side, fighting against the bad."

"In this day and age, it's a tough job," Cody says.

"It's changed a lot over the years. When I first started, I saw everything in black and white, right or wrong. Now I see life in various shades of gray."

"When did you have the accident?" he asks.

"Three years ago."

"When did the seizures start?"

"Immediately following the accident. My doctors don't seem to be able to control them with medication yet. Right now, I can get one at any time. There are no signs or warnings. I only know I had one when I wake up."

"So, how can a service dog help you?" Cody asks.

"I was hoping you could answer that for me," I answer.

"It surprises people to know that most dogs have the ability to detect seizures. There are two theories out there that try to explain how. One is that the dog senses a subtle change in a person's behavior. The other is that the dog has the ability to pick up a change in the person's body odor."

"Being alerted to a seizure would benefit my life greatly. I wouldn't end up so sore from all the falls. With some warning, I could immediately sit or lie down. What are my chances that a dog could do this for me?" I ask.

"The hard part is encouraging the dog to recognize the seizure and alert its owner. We have three dogs in service right now who are doing just that. They started out just providing assistance, but over a period of time, each one of them learned to alert its owner to upcoming seizures. There are no guarantees, though."

"It's a chance I would like to take."

"Would you be able and willing to take care of all the expenses and needs of the dog?" Cody asks.

"Money would not be a problem," I respond.

"Did you get a settlement from the accident?"

"Yes, I did."

Cody looks over at Alfie, and I see her nod. She goes to a file cabinet and returns with a packet of papers.

"This is the formal application packet. You need to follow all its instructions and return it to us."

"Then what happens?" I ask.

"When your application is complete, we will call you and arrange for a home visit."

"I live four hours away."

"That's not a problem," Cody replies. "We just need to make sure you can provide a safe environment for the dog."

"That I can do. We can take care of each other."

"Then the waiting begins. We will notify you when we feel we have a dog that will be a good match for you."

"Do you have any idea how long?"

"No. We have a long list, and we never know the individual traits of our dogs until they join us for advanced training," Cody answers. "You will need to be patient."

After the interview, I decide to walk down the lane while I wait for MJ to pick me up. I realize that I forgot how great it is to be in the company of a dog. Before today, I still had my doubts. After this interview, I can now see the possibilities. Just maybe I can picture myself walking through life with a dog by my side.

Chapter 5

Haley Duncan

We both shake off the rain as I hang up Chance's harness. April showers, boy, they got that right. While I'm putting him back in his kennel, I hear the door slam and see Cody approaching me.

"Haley, just the person I've been looking for. I need to talk to you."

"Alfie told me to take Chance for a walk. We just got back."

"No problem. Come with me."

I follow Cody into his office, and he closes the door behind me.

"Did I do something wrong?" I ask.

"No, no. It's nothing like that. I want you to meet someone."

He goes over to the crate beside his desk and opens the door. A very young black Lab comes bounding out and races over to greet me. Our feet become tangled, and as I steady myself, he proceeds to jump all over me.

"Hey, buddy . . . relax . . . I'm petting you. Come on, four on the floor. That's a good boy, or is it girl?" I say, looking up at Cody.

"Boy, meet Jed. He's the reason I need to talk to you."

"Do you want me to work with him today? It's only three o'clock. I can give you some more time?"

"Haley, take a seat. I want to talk to you about Jed," Cody says as he corners Jed and puts the squirming dog back in the crate. Immediately Jed starts to whimper and scratch the door, not at all happy with this change of events.

"He's a lively one, isn't he?" I say.

"You have that right. I'm hoping you can help us out. Jed is kind of an emergency."

"Do you need me to take him to the vet?"

"No. It's worse than that. His puppy raiser is Stella Wagner. Do you know her from volunteering?"

"No. I don't."

"Stella got sick very shortly after Jed was placed with her. Being a single lady with no family around, she was having trouble taking care of herself, let alone raising Jed. As a result, he's missed most of his puppy classes, and he's fallen way behind the other puppies from his litter. This last week, Stella was diagnosed with stage four breast cancer. She is facing surgery, then chemo, and who knows what else. She has to move out of state to live with her sister as she battles this."

"I'm sorry to hear that. I hate cancer!"

"Stella is adamant that her cancer not hurt Jed any more than it already has. Although I've assured her that I won't let that happen, I can't find an immediate placement for him. I have been searching through all our normal channels, and nothing is working out. We need someone *now*." He pauses, looking intently at me. "I thought of you."

"What? Me? No! I can't do this. I'm not your answer."

"We really need your help here, Haley. It might only be until his six-month evaluation. That's just two months from now. If he doesn't somehow get turned around, he won't pass, and we'll have to dismiss him from the program."

"Cody, I appreciate all your confidence in me, but . . ."

"All the trainers agree you're a natural around the dogs. We're really hoping you'll do this. It's Jed's only chance."

"I . . . I just don't know. This is so sudden."

"I know it's a lot to ask on such short notice."

"Doesn't a puppy raiser have to have special training?"

"You already know most of the stuff from volunteering."

"What more does it entail?"

"You've raised a puppy before. Just give him lots of exercise and new experiences, attend the puppy classes, teach him his manners, take him to school with you, and most of all, love him."

"But I have two dogs at home. I don't know how they will react."

"I bet they will be good role models for this little guy."

"Well . . . ah . . . how old is he now?"

"Jed just turned four months. He'll be evaluated in June."

"If he passes his six-month evaluation, then it would be another six months until advanced training, right?" I ask.

"We can only hope," Cody replies.

"I don't know if I can do this."

"I think you can, Haley, and all the trainers here will be with you every step of the way. Jed deserves his chance."

"I know he does, but . . ."

"He's a work in progress," Cody says.

"Aren't we all?" I answer.

"Will you do it?"

"I need time . . . Time to wrap my head around all this," I say.

"The trouble is Jed doesn't have time. He's lost so much of it already. Listen. Don't give me an answer right now. He's staying with me this weekend, but I can't keep him very long. I'm already raising a puppy. Tomorrow is Sunday. Think it over. Give me a call tomorrow night with your answer."

"That I can do," I say as I get up to leave.

"And, Haley?"

"Yes?"

"I have a feeling about Jed. He's going to be a special dog if he's given a chance."

I don't respond. I look over at Jed in the crate. He has his head resting between his paws, but he's not sleeping. Those big brown eyes are looking at me. No, they're looking deep inside me as if he knows that I won't let him down.

After school on Monday, I again find myself in Cody's office.

"I think you have everything. Crate, food bowl, collar with his ID tag, lead, harness, and oh yes, his toy duck."

"All I need is Jed," I say.

"I'll go get him," says Cody.

It's hard not to smile as Jed races into the room and almost knocks me over with his greeting.

"Hey Jed, are you ready to go home with me?"

"I'm really glad you decided to do this, Haley."

"To tell you the truth, I still can't believe I am. When I left here on Saturday, I thought I would be hashing out the pros and cons all evening. Instead, I found myself puppy-proofing the house."

"You're a special person, Haley, and I feel, given a chance, Jed is going to be a special dog. I'll see the two of you on Thursday for puppy class."

"We'll be there."

On the way home, I keep looking over my shoulder and taking a quick glance at Jed. He is curled up in his crate, sleeping away, unaware that he is heading to a new home. Every time I look at him, I find myself shaking my head, wondering what I'm doing. Why is it always so hard for me to say no to people? I don't even have him home yet, and already I can feel my mothering instincts kicking in. It's not going to be hard for me to make room for him in my heart. I just wonder how welcoming Magic and Thunder will be.

I would have preferred introducing Magic and Thunder to Jed by scent, not sight, but I don't have the luxury of time. Jed's lucky they're two golden retrievers who love everybody and everything. Leaving him in the car, I enter the house.

"Magic, Thunder, sit." Four big brown eyes are focused on me, waiting for their treat, tails thumping.

"Stay, Thunder." I grab Magic's collar and lead her into the kitchen and out the dog door, blocking it behind her.

"OK, Thunder." I give him a quick hug when he gets up. I return to the car, pick Jed up in my arms, and head for the backyard. Within a minute, Magic comes barreling over to us. After treating her, I slowly start to walk around the yard. As Jed wiggles in my arms, Magic races around us, darting from side to side. "Relax, Magic. I know you're excited. Come on, calm down."

I gradually make my way over to the bench in the corner of the yard, where I sit down with Jed on my lap. Immediately Magic puts her head on my lap and sniffs Jed. When some squirrels in the yard distract her, I put Jed down but keep him on a leash. Magic comes bounding back over and sniffs Jed from head to toe.

"Take it easy, girl. He's a lot smaller than you." I breathe a huge sigh of relief when she starts licking his head.

The three of us walk around the yard together. I keep my eyes on Jed, hoping that he will get the idea and do his business. After a while, with no success, I head for the house. Leaving Magic outside, I repeat the same process inside with Thunder.

I am always fascinated by dog behavior. True to his personality, Thunder's introduction to Jed is much calmer than Magic's. "Thunder, you're the top dog around here. What do you think? Should we keep him?" I ask him. Things go pretty smoothly, and I realize it's OK to let Magic back in.

As I open the dog door for Magic and start to take off my coat, I turn back around and see Jed wetting in the middle of the kitchen.

"No, Jed. Thunder, leave it. Magic, come." Both dogs ignore me, proceed to walk through the puddle on the floor, and follow Jed as he scampers toward me.

"What have I done?" I say to myself as I pick Jed up and head outside with three smelly dogs.

Checking my phone as the dogs wander around the backyard, I see a missed call from Cassie. I think about whether I want to talk to my sister right now. I know she's just checking up on me again. I hit the recall button. As I keep an eye on Jed, I hear the call go to voice mail. "Figures," I mutter.

Sitting down on the bench, I find myself thinking about my sister. Cassie and I are four years apart, and we couldn't be more different. Although we share many of the same physical features, our personalities vary greatly, and so do our lives. She and Mike have four children, and sometimes that makes things difficult between us—at least for me, it does.

Punching redial, I try calling her again.

"Hey, Cassie." Hearing a door slam, I pause before asking, "Is this a bad time?"

"Nope, just putting the casserole in the oven," she answers.

"I haven't even figured out what I'm going to eat."

"And this is a hard thing to do?"

"It was never hard before," I admit.

"I don't know how you do it. I hate eating alone," she says.

"I wish I could be like my dogs. They eat the same meal every day and are as happy as can be. All those years when I found cooking to be such a chore . . . now I miss someone to cook for."

"Well, you should try cooking for six every night," she says.

When I don't respond, Cassie says, "Haley, I'm sorry. I didn't mean to say that."

"It's OK. Don't worry about it."

"I think I heard a car horn. Are you driving somewhere?" she asks.

"No. I'm in my backyard. It came from the neighborhood."

"You sound sad."

"Really, I don't mean to."

"Hey, this is me you're talking to. How are you really doing?"

"I'm doing OK, a little lonely at times, but OK. I've started keeping the TV or music on, so it seems like there is someone in the house with me."

"That seems like a good idea. I don't know how you do it. I could never deal with that kind of silence. I wish I lived closer."

"Me too."

"Thank goodness for my dogs . . . and thank goodness for my teaching. School keeps me focused and busy, so there is not much time to dwell on things during the day. I wish I could say the same thing about the evenings. Even though I am usually grading papers, the nights are still the worst. I don't know what it is about the darkness."

"The dogs should help make that big house less empty."

"Did I ever tell you that I had to deal with Thunder and Magic's grief, too?" I add.

"Come on, Haley."

"No, really, I'm not making this up."

"You never mentioned it, and that is something I would have remembered. Are you sure you were not projecting your own feelings on your dogs?"

"I wouldn't have believed it if I hadn't seen it myself. For the longest time after Jack died, they just lay around."

"Haley, that's what dogs do."

"No, this was different. Both of them didn't seem to have any energy. They didn't even care to play together, and you know how much they love to do that. It seemed like they watched me all the time . . . and followed me from room to room more than normal . . . and they whined every time I left the house. It almost broke my heart."

"OK. Look, I'm sure they missed Jack's presence in the house. After all, he loved them too."

"Don't worry, I didn't share this with many people. They might think I'd lost it entirely. My friends with dogs understood completely, though. I was so thankful that I had them to talk to. Anyway, it took a couple of months, but Magic and Thunder bounced back to normal. I wish it was that easy for people."

"Give it time."

"Like I haven't heard that before."

Cassie doesn't respond to this, and after a moment, I add, "I have something else to tell you. Do you remember me talking about the Homeland Service Dog Association, where I volunteer?"

"Of course I do. You raved about them for the last two years."

"Well, they need an emergency puppy raiser, and they've asked me to do it."

"What? Haley, are you crazy?"

"Not that I'm aware of."

"You can't be serious! After all that you've been through, this is not a good idea!"

"I agree with you."

"You can't raise a puppy and then give it away. I know you, Haley. Look, you say a prayer for every animal you see killed along the road. You bury dead birds and rabbits you find in your yard. You carry carrots in your car to feed the horse down the road that you feel doesn't get any attention. You don't need this after everything you've gone through."

"I know. I totally agree with you."

"Well, I'm glad that's settled."

"His name is Jed, and he is roaming my backyard as we speak."

"Haley, this is so bad for you on so many levels," Cassie says.

"Do you think I don't know that?"

"So why is there a puppy in your backyard?"

"It was an emergency. His puppy raiser got cancer. I couldn't say no."

"Haley, you need to say no to this. You will fall in love with this puppy, and it will devastate you when you have to give it up."

"You're right. But for the last two years, I felt like I was just going through the motions of living. Maybe Jed is exactly what I need to shake things up. Life hasn't been fair to him either."

"And what happens if you're wrong?"

"I'll survive. It seems like I'm getting a lot of practice at grieving."

"Why ask for more?"

"Because I think by making a difference in this puppy's life, he will make a difference in mine."

We are both quiet now. Finally, Cassie says, "I still think this is wrong for you."

"I know, and you're probably right."

"Please don't let me have to say I told you so. Wait, I'm sorry. Pretend you didn't hear that. I didn't mean it, but I really feel you're thinking with your heart here instead of your head."

"Listen, Cassie. I'm doing this. Hopefully, I can turn this puppy around and give him a chance of making it through his six-month evaluation. Right now, that's a long shot." As I watch Jed sprinting around the yard, jumping and barking at Magic, I can't help but add, "He's going to be a challenge."

"If this puppy doesn't make it, I'm sure it will be no fault of yours. You are good at everything you set out to do," Cassie adds.

"That's not true, but I could use your support."

"Always, even though I don't always agree with you, especially about this. Raising a service dog . . ." She pauses, and although she is three states away in Boston, I can hear her sigh. "This has heartbreak written all over it. I just don't want to see you hurt again."

"I know."

I am still thinking about our conversation as I herd the dogs into the house. When I see Jed's puddle on the kitchen floor, I give Cassie a final thought. What if she's right?

CHAPTER 6

MARK LANCER

“ Dad, when was the last time you played golf?” MJ asks as he takes a practice swing in the small patch of grass in front of the condo.

“Since before the accident,” I respond.

“It’s definitely time to get you back out there.”

“Oh, I don’t know, MJ.”

“Come on, Dad. It’s a beautiful August day. My month is almost up, and I haven’t been able to get you out on the course yet. Give me something to gloat about before I leave.”

“I don’t want to give you nightmares.”

“If you have a seizure, I’ll just drag you into the rough and tell anyone going by that we’re looking for your golf ball.”

“Very funny.”

“You’re just afraid I’ll beat you.”

“Now that I’m not afraid of.”

“Come on. It will be like old times.”

“Let’s not mention time. If you give up your plan of backpacking all over Europe after your semester abroad, we would have a month next summer, too,” I say.

"I can't miss that opportunity, Dad. I don't know when I'll ever have a chance like that again."

"You're right. I'm just giving you a hard time. I want you to have a great experience. Just make sure you come back safe. Are you still planning on applying to that med school that's all the way across the country?"

"The University of California–San Francisco is one of the top schools of medicine in the United States. I really hope they accept me. The only drawback is that Pittsburgh is so far away."

"How did I end up getting the short end of the stick? Your mother's probably within walking distance."

"I know. Ironic, isn't it?" MJ says.

"I guess I won't see much of you this next year."

"You know I'll keep in touch. You're just a text or call away," MJ says.

Handing me the golf club, I follow his lead and take a few practice swings. "Tell me something, MJ. Was my accident and seizures the motivation behind you going to med school?"

"Part of it, I guess, but I've always been fascinated by the workings of the human body. Plus, like you, I want to help people."

"I'm not helping a lot of people now."

"Yes, you are. Somebody has to do the behind-the-scenes stuff," MJ says.

Getting the putter out of his bag, MJ drops two golf balls on the grass. "Let's see who can hit that leaf from here," he says.

"You're on. Putting was always your weakness."

"That's because you were always talking or dropping clubs to ruin my concentration."

"I was just working on your mental toughness."

"Right," MJ says as his putt goes to the right off the leaf.

"Give me that putter, and I'll show you how to do it."

"Lucky," MJ mumbles as my golf ball rolls over its mark.

"Now, let's give credit where credit is due," I say with a smirk.

As we continue to challenge each other's putting skills using various objects in the front yard, MJ asks, "So, how are you doing with the new medication?"

"Well, I'm not having any side effects," I answer.

"That's not what I meant, and you know it," MJ says.

"I had a seizure last night when you were out with your friends. No big deal. I was just watching TV, and when I came out of it, the only damage done was that I missed the end of the evening news."

"Damn, I was hoping the new meds would work."

"Me too, but they warned me my body would need time to get used to them."

"It's been a week."

"Hey, I'm trying to be optimistic here."

"Sorry, Dad. Have you heard anything more about the service dog?"

"You mean since last week when you asked me?"

The look MJ gives me reminds me so much of my father that I can't help laughing. "It could take years, MJ."

"Are you having second thoughts?"

"No, but don't get your hopes up. The trainers warned me that even when it's my turn, it could take several tries to find a good match."

"Dad, lose your street cop attitude and turn on the charm."

"This isn't a dating situation."

"You dating, that I would like to see!"

"Right. What woman would want to date me?"

"Are you crazy? What woman wouldn't want to date you?"

"Your mother."

"She's the exception."

"I can't drive. What would I do, ask my date to walk to dinner?"

"Not an issue. She'll drive. Women love to feel needed."

"Since when did you become an expert on women?"

"I think I've had a couple more girlfriends than you, Dad."

"OK, enough. I almost feel sorry for those college women."

"You're going to feel sorry for yourself when I destroy you on the golf course. I'm going inside and booking us a tee time tomorrow. That way, when I beat you, there is still time for another round before I go."

As I put our clubs in the trunk for tomorrow's game, I wonder what I would do without MJ in my life. The only good thing that came out of my accident is that he won't have to worry about any student loans. For that, I'm glad. Even though it's been years since the accident, I still miss my old life. I should be moving on, but I feel stuck, and when I look ahead, I can't see it getting any better.

CHAPTER 7

HALEY DUNCAN

"Are you ready to go?" I ask as I stick my head in Lynn's classroom. I love her room. It's colorful and welcoming, just like she is.

"I'm ready. I was just waiting for you," she says. From the stack of papers on her desk, I can see she was busy grading while she waited.

"No Jed today?" she asks.

"No, he's at the vet. It's that time."

"Oh boy, he's going to be mad at you."

"He will be healthier and, in the long run, happier," I say.

"Aren't you glad he can't talk?"

"If he could, I would have done a better job at explaining it to him. I remember Jack and I waited too long to fix our first dog. When the neighbor's dog went into heat, Dewey was a basket case, howling and carrying on like you wouldn't believe. He even broke through our screen door, trying to get to her. Thank goodness they kept her under lock and key."

"That's a male for you. When do you pick him up?"

"Around six. Are you taking a sweatshirt? September isn't usually this cold," I say.

"No. We walk fast," she replies.

"Do you have time for a one-hour walk today?" I ask as I set my watch.

"Hey, my time is my time. Luke's away on business for the week, so it's just me. I'm not the one who has three dogs waiting at home," she says.

"I really think we have to do something about that. There is some poor animal out there just waiting for you to break down and give it a good home."

"I know you're right. Someday it will happen, but not right now. Luke's away so much, and when I can, I like to travel with him. It wouldn't be fair to the animal."

"You know I could always help you with that."

"Oh, ye of the kind heart! Right now, I am content enjoying everybody else's pets. So tell me, what's going on with Jed?"

"You know, when I got him, I thought I knew some things about dog training. It didn't take me long to find out I had a lot to learn. I don't know who's getting more of an education, Jed or me."

"So, are you teaching him to open doors and answer phones yet?"

"No," I respond. "That's advanced training if he makes it that far. At this stage in his life, we are working on his manners and a variety of basic cues."

"How's it going?"

"Well, it's going. Jed needs to be kept busy. If he has any downtime, he gets into trouble. I just noticed that he's been chewing on the legs of my kitchen chairs and table. Here I thought he was doing such a good job of staying down while I ate. He's really smart and learns quickly. Unfortunately, it's not always the things he should learn. His jumping up on people and counter-surfing is better, which is a good thing since he's going to be a big dog when he's fully grown. But if he were one of my students, I would have to fail him on loose leash walking. Every night, we walk around the block working on his leash skills. Right now, he's up to twenty steps without pulling, and that's with a treat in my hand."

"I bet Magic and Thunder are bent out of shape when they can't go along."

"You got that right."

"But he's still young," Lynn says.

"He'll turn a year next month," I respond.

"What do the trainers say at those classes you attend?"

"I don't know how he's managed to do it, but he's passed all his temperament and health tests so far. I think the trainers felt sorry for both of us and cut him a break. If he manages to continue making progress, the next step is advanced training. If he does complete the program, he'll have to be carefully matched."

"Aren't they all?"

"Some are easier than others. The trainers will determine the job that suits him best and then custom-train him for it. He's a big-sized Lab, so that might mean balance work. Maybe he'll help a veteran or someone with a movement disability. If they find he's good at tracking, it might mean an autistic child who has a tendency to run away. It will be really interesting to see with whom he's matched . . . if he makes it that far."

"I don't know how you do it," she says.

"Jed's a work in progress. He's my homework I do every day. Just like teaching, this is another labor of love."

"Well, the kids love him. They rush out of my room at the end of class so they can stop and see him."

"I know. I'm waiting for Principal Richards to call me in and reprimand me for all the 'Jed' passes I'm writing."

"How's he doing during your classes?"

"He's better behaved than some of my students. They are always begging me to let him out of his crate so they can pet him during class. They inform me they can listen better this way. I use a little bribery of my own. If the entire class turns in their homework for the day, I let him out for the last five minutes of the period. The interaction is good for everyone."

"Maybe I should borrow him and try that. Some of my students could use some motivation," Lynn says.

"It's fun being able to take him everywhere with me," I say.

"Have you had any problems with that yet?"

"I haven't, but some of the other puppy raisers have. In this day and age, most people are pretty well educated about the Americans with Disabilities Act."

"You know, Haley, this experience has been good for you. I was worried at first when you told me about it, but I can see that Jed has breathed new life into you."

"This has been a greater challenge than I expected. Although Jack and I trained three dogs together, it was a hit-or-miss process. They each had their own individual quirks. With Jed, there is a whole program that I have to follow to give him the best chance of success."

"What happens if he doesn't make it?"

"Don't even say that. Everybody keeps reminding me that if he doesn't work out, I get to keep him. While it's true that I would have first choice of ownership, I really want Jed to be a success story."

"How much longer do you have him?" Lynn asks.

"If all goes according to schedule, he will leave for advanced training in February, less than four months away."

"Is that it? Will you ever get to see him again?" she asks.

"Yes. He'll live at the kennel for the week, but I'll still have him on weekends and holidays. It's a gradual goodbye."

I look at my watch as we finish the loop. "It's been an hour already. I'm sorry I talked your ear off. That's what happens when you live alone," I say.

"Don't apologize. It was great to hear you open up for a change. Usually, I'm the one talking, and you're the one listening. You know I'm cheering for you and Jed."

"Thanks. He will need it these next few months. Are you on for Thursday?" I ask.

"That should work," Lynn answers.

We are quiet as we enter the school and walk to the English wing. As we split to go to our classrooms, I say to Lynn, "You've been a great friend to me. I want you to know how much I value you in my life."

Surprised, she gives me a hug. "Me too."

"You know, I never found the right moment to tell Jack some things that I really wanted him to know. I was wrong to think that there was plenty of time. I vowed to myself that I would not make that mistake again."

"Don't you dare give up teaching and go be a dog trainer on me. I would be lost here without you," Lynn says.

I laugh and say, "Not a chance."

"Or some guy comes along and sweeps you off your feet and takes you away from here," she adds.

"Like that's going to happen," I say.

"I'm surprised it hasn't happened already. See you tomorrow on hall duty."

"Jed and I will be there bright and early. Or at least I'll be there bright and early. I don't know how Jed's going to be feeling."

Finding a best friend right down the hall is a bonus I didn't expect when I was hired here. Back then, I took it for granted. Sixteen years later, I need her friendship more than ever.

———————————————————

"Jed, car."

I can't help but laugh as he uses those big paws to hurdle himself into the back seat. When the rest of his body fills out and catches up to those paws, he could be a sight to behold. As I get in and start the engine, I can see Magic and Thunder glaring at us through the front window. I feel a pang of guilt as we drive away. They don't understand that Jed is permitted in places that they aren't. He needs as many new experiences as possible for his successful development.

As I pull into the cell lot at the airport, I feel myself smiling as I take a glance back at Jed. I won't tell Cassie or anyone else, but Jed's brought out my maternal instincts. This might be as close as I have ever come to being a mother.

At Cassie's text, I head over to the pickup area. I notice that Jed is watching a plane land. "Who knows, Jed, you might be flying some day and not in the cargo area either."

I see Cassie waving to us from the curb. True to form, she is talking to the couple waiting next to her. She has always been such a people person. I barely get the car stopped, and she is opening the door and greeting both of us.

"How was your flight?" I ask.

"A little bumpy going up, but then it smoothed out. It's really an easy flight. I hardly had enough time to down my drink and play some word games," she said.

"What did it take, a little over two hours?"

"That's about right."

"How are Mike and the kids?" I ask.

"Good to both. You know, I hit the jackpot when I met Mike. He is so good at letting me be me. It was his idea that I visit you this weekend."

"Cassie, you know you didn't have to come. I'm fine."

"It's more for my peace of mind than yours," she answers.

"I feel like I'm keeping you from your family."

"What? You're my sister. You don't consider yourself my family?"

"Of course I do. You know what I mean."

"Quit worrying. Mike's parents were overjoyed at the chance of visiting and spending the weekend with him and the kids. I'm not sure which they like better: taking care of their son again or spoiling their grandchildren."

"I'm sure it's a little of both."

"Either way, I'm here now, and we have the weekend. Can I pet Jed?"

"Yes. Jed, sit. Remember, it's not really goodbye yet. Even though Jed leaves for advanced training next Sunday, I still have him for weekends and holidays."

"I know, you told me. Can I help it if I wanted to see for myself how you're doing? I guess this visit is more for me than for you," she answers.

"Don't get me wrong, it's nice to have you here, but I'm fine, really."

"Sure, you'll endure like you always do. You are so good at hiding your feelings."

"That's not true."

"Is too."

"Lately, I've been trying to break that habit," I say.

"That's a step in the right direction," Cassie adds. "So, is Jed the perfect dog yet?"

"Far from it. But he's made a lot of progress. I just hope he continues to improve in advanced training. He can still be dismissed from the program if things don't work out there."

"Well, then you'll end up with three dogs, and I don't have anything to worry about."

"And all my work would have been for nothing," I say.

"You know that's not true. You will have a very well-trained dog who likes to pull you around the neighborhood."

"And Magic and Thunder will be very happy. Now that Jed is growing into his body, they have another playmate."

"You talk about your dogs the way I talk about my kids."

"They are my kids."

"That's something I'll have to remember."

I pull into the little family-owned Italian restaurant around the block from my house. Cassie and I like to eat here when she visits. We both like the homey atmosphere, and they are so good with Jed. They always seat me at a table with plenty of room for him to spread out.

"Cassie, don't you dare drop any tidbits under the table for Jed."

"I wouldn't think of it."

"Right. All those years growing up together, I know how you think."

"Accidents happen, Haley."

"And dropping snacks to Jed is not one of them."

"OK, I got it."

"Have you talked to Mom and Dad lately?" I ask.

"Last week. They are loving being out of this cold weather," she answers.

"I haven't been calling them as much as I should. It always seems like they're lecturing me."

"That's something we share. I wonder if my kids say that about me," she says.

After we discuss the menu and order our meals, I look across the table at my sister, and our years apart seem to fade away. "Tell me one of your best memories growing up," I ask.

"Wow, where did that come from?" Cassie asks.

"Maybe it's talking about Mom and Dad or this place," I respond.

"Boy, I'll have to think about that one."

"I'll answer it first," I say. "I remember how you used to sneak over to my room at night even though we each had our own bedrooms. We would talk and giggle until the wee hours of the morning. I never told you how special that made me feel."

"I remember that. I hated being alone. I always wanted to be with you. You were always so much fun. Do you remember the camping trip Dad took us on? Mom wouldn't go because she hated bugs. I remember how great it felt to have Dad all to ourselves for the weekend," Cassie says.

"How about when Mom and Dad took that trip for their twenty-fifth wedding anniversary and Aunt Sue and Grandma came and stayed with us? We laughed all week," I add with a chuckle.

"Especially at the stories Grandma told us about Mom," Cassie responds, joining in with my laughter.

"Do you remember Mom taking us shopping for my first prom dress? I liked the first one I tried on, but she made us look in every store at the mall before she would buy that one for me."

"I loved that day. The whole time I was dreaming of myself in my prom dress someday. I always wished you could have shopped for my first one with me," she replies.

"Sorry, I never knew that."

"It was OK. You were away at school."

"I could have come home. All you had to do was ask."

"I know you would have. That's why I didn't. Do you—"

"Sorry," I interrupt when I feel Jed's head on my lap. "Jed, down, stay." He looks at me, circles, and settles back down. "That's something they're going to have to work on in advanced training," I tell Cassie.

"I was saying, do you remember how Grandpa made up that song so we could memorize the books of the Bible?"

"Acts, Amos, Chronicles, Colossians," I sing.

"Corinthians, Daniel, Deuteronomy," Cassie adds. We stop after we notice the people at the next table are looking at us strangely. It feels good to laugh together over the same memory.

"Some things you never forget," I say.

"I taught it to my kids. I really hope they pass it down to their children," Cassie adds.

"You know, I told Mom one day that you were the best present she ever gave me."

Cassie looks up from her food. "Really, you did? She never told me."

"I meant it then, and I mean it now," I say.

"That could be the most beautiful thing anyone has ever said to me." Cassie gets up from her chair, walks around the table, and gives me a heartfelt hug. "I always thought you were perfect, you know," she says.

"Well, I had you fooled," I answer, smiling.

It's nice having this time for just the two of us. I feel closer to Cassie than I have in a long time. Even though our lives move in such different circles, you can't change the past. We will always have that connection. There are certain times in life when you know you are making memories. Sitting across from my sister, with Jed under my feet, I realize that this is one of them.

CHAPTER 8

MARK LANCER

May is such a month of promise. Looking out the bus window on the last leg of my journey, I hope this trip will be full of promise too. When the call came from the Homeland Service Dog Association, it caught me off guard.

"Mark, can you come out and meet a few dogs?" Cody asked. "Keep in mind that there is no guarantee that you'll get matched. Sometimes it takes several attempts."

"Name the day, and I'll be there," I answered. Next month will be a year and a half since my first interview. Maybe my luck is changing. Things are moving faster than usual.

I haven't talked to anyone about this except MJ. Although my sergeant and fellow officers have been very supportive, I'm waiting until this is a sure thing. They would be asking all kinds of questions for which I have few answers. As the bus slows to a stop at the station, I am already getting out of my seat when the bus driver says, "Sir, this is your stop."

"Thanks," I reply. I had to let the driver know about my seizures since I'm traveling alone. I feel like I should just wear a sign around my neck: "Caution: Seizures!" After exiting the bus station, I look around for my ride.

"Mark Lancer?" a frail, older gentleman asks.

"That's me," I reply.

"Brad Parker, one of Homeland's volunteers."

"I appreciate the ride."

"My pleasure."

I get into his F-250 pickup truck. I am surprised to see a man of his age driving this type of vehicle. He pulls out of the parking lot and starts driving away from the town. "Nice ride," I say.

"Don't think I could manage without my truck," he replies.

"When I was here for my interview, we came a different way."

"I lived here all my life, so I know the back roads. I hear you're here for a possible match."

"That's the plan."

"I work with most of the dogs, and they're all great. I hope it works out for you."

"Thanks, so do I."

When we arrive at the kennel, another volunteer escorts me to an office to wait. "You're a little early," she says. "The trainers are finishing up with another client. Make yourself comfortable."

Glancing around the room, I see pictures of service dogs covering most of the available wall space. There are file cabinets lined up against the wall to my left. I bet the stories of all the service dogs and their clients are found in them. I take a seat in the corner to wait.

"Mark. Hi. Sorry, we kept you waiting," Cody says as he shakes my hand. "How was your trip?"

"Fine. I appreciate you sending Brad to pick me up."

"We have great volunteers. He's hanging around so he can take you back."

"I'll pay for his gas."

"You can offer, but I doubt he'll accept. Are you ready?" When he sees me nod, he says, "Follow me." He leads me into a large gathering room, and he asks me to take a seat. "We're going to videotape this session. Are you OK with that?"

"No problem," I respond as I notice a lady in the far corner with a camera.

"We have three dogs we'd like you to meet today. I believe you met Alfie at your first interview?"

"I did," I respond.

"She will bring the dogs in one at a time. Just interact with them, talk to them, pet them, get a feel for them. Any questions?"

"No, I'm ready," I answer.

"The first one is a female named Sugar," Cody says.

Alfie brings in a small yellow Lab and releases her from the leash. Sugar walks over to me, and I squat down to say hello. True to her name, she is sweet as can be with big chocolate eyes that don't seem to miss anything. Cody and Alfie are quiet and give me time to get to know her a bit.

"Sugar, come," Alfie says. Sugar immediately turns from me and trots back to Alfie. "I'll be back," she says.

"The next dog is a male named Jed," Cody says as Alfie leads a big black Lab into the room and removes his leash.

Jed dashes over to say hello. "Hey, Jed, you're a big boy," I say to him as I pet him under his chin. Jed stands in front of me, watching me closely. It makes me feel like he knows something I don't. He has a presence about him that draws me in. Then again, maybe it's just his size.

"Jed, come," Alfie says. Jed gives me one more look, turns quickly, and returns to Alfie.

The last dog I meet is a yellow Lab bigger than Sugar but not as big as Jed.

"This is River," Cody says.

River seems a bit of a clown and is very playful. He makes low whining sounds as I pet him. It's almost like he's talking to me. I can't help but laugh at some of his expressions. I can see how this dog would be a lot of fun.

"River, come," Alfie says. River immediately gets up from his belly rub and returns to her. She puts his leash on and leads him away.

"Well, Mark, what do you think?" Cody asks.

"They're all impressive."

"Could you be more specific?"

"I would probably lean toward the males. I just like the bigger size. I liked River's personality. He's a real charmer. Jed's full of energy. He exudes confidence, as if he's the top dog. His eyes seem like they can look right through you."

"You have good instincts. It must be the cop in you," Cody says.

"Do you think these three have what it takes to help me with my seizures?" I ask.

"We think they might," Cody replies. "Our team of trainers will review the tapes of the session and discuss placement options for all five of the clients that came in today. We'll let you know one way or the other what we decide. Please keep in mind if you aren't matched today, you will have other opportunities."

"I appreciate the chance. You do amazing work here with these dogs."

I shake Cody's hand and exit the building, still thinking about the three dogs I met today. Heading to the parking lot, I hear barking coming from a fenced-in yard. Dogs are playing, and I am drawn to their exuberance. There must be ten Labs: yellows, blacks, and even a brown. Leaning against the fence, I watch them delight in the freedom of their play. Each one of them will spend their life changing the lives of people like me. It's a humbling thought. I hope I'm worthy.

CHAPTER 9

HALEY DUNCAN

As I watch the three dogs eat, I find it hard to believe that this is the last weekend that Jed will be home with us. The dogs finish their meals in their usual order: Jed, Magic, then Thunder. As Thunder and Magic check bowls in hopes of finding some missed tidbit, I call Jed over to me.

"Down."

As he plops down at my feet, my other two, who are done with their forage, come and do the same. I talk softly to him as I run my hand over his back and under his chin. "Tomorrow, you'll be leaving us for good. When you're gone, there will be an emptiness in this house that all of us will feel."

I push back the kitchen chair and head for the door. "Jed, come."

Magic and Thunder follow Jed's lead, and we all head for the backyard. It is one of those beautiful August nights. The sky is so dark and clear that you feel like you can touch the stars. As the dogs wander around, I think back on the day. It was a great last day together. I took them for their favorite walk and let them swim in the creek. Three wet dogs—what a mess and what a joy! They continually remind me to appreciate the simple pleasures in life.

I walk back to the deck and take a seat. Within a few minutes, all three dogs join me, settling down near my feet. As I glance at each one of them, it strikes me that in choosing their various spots, Thunder and Magic put Jed in the middle. Their golden color is in stark contrast to his black coat. I feel blessed, and I wish this moment in time could be repeated again and again.

The trainers did wonders with Jed in advanced training. He flourished and matured under their guidance. I'm so proud of the dog he's become. I hope his new owner realizes how special he is. As bad as I feel right now, raising Jed was a good decision. He's made a difference in my life, and now he will make a difference in someone else's. It's time for me to let him go. It strikes me that I've had to do a lot of letting go in my life. It's been a hard lesson to learn, and I wish my life story could have been different.

Tomorrow I will drop him off, and he will begin his two-week training with his new owner. As a volunteer, I could have assisted with team training or provided lunch, but I feel it would be counterproductive. I didn't want Jed to be distracted or confused if I were in attendance. Although I hope to meet Jed's new owner someday, my job as a puppy raiser is completed. Now it's Jed's time to become the working dog he was raised to be.

A few days ago, there was an opportunity for me to still contribute. Cody sent out an email to all volunteers, asking for anyone willing to transport one of the clients to and from training every day. For whatever reason, this client does not have his own transportation available. I thought it would be a great opportunity to help out. I'm on summer break from school, so I have the time. This will give me the chance to feel close to Jed for a little while longer.

Monday morning will find me outside the Marriott Suites at 8:30 a.m., ready to provide a taxi service. All I know is that his name is Mark Lancer, and he will be waiting for me.

Chapter 10

Mark Lancer

"I knew you'd never ask, so I decided to take care of your transportation to your training," Greg says. "We state troopers like to take care of our own."

"Greg, I don't want you taking the day away from your family just to chauffeur me," I say.

"I knew you would say that, but I don't want to see you taking the bus four hours across the state like you did before."

"Just trying to support public transportation," I reply.

"I wish I could do it personally, but it's our shore week. Instead, I made arrangements with fellow troopers to form a station-to-station relay for you."

"You're kidding," I say.

"Not a chance. We're out on the highways on a Sunday anyway. I had plenty of volunteers from the different stations. I think you'll enjoy this more than the bus," Greg says.

The outpouring of help and support I continually receive humbles me. I hate to be this kind of bother to anyone, even though my friends and total strangers are falling all over themselves to help.

Greg was right. I really enjoyed meeting the cops in the relay, and they delivered me to the Marriott, where I'm staying for the next two weeks. I just finished their complimentary breakfast. Not having to leave the hotel will make my mornings a lot easier. Conveniently, I don't have to worry about lunch since it's provided at the training session. Supper is a different story. The desk clerk informed me that I'm within walking distance of a string of fast-food restaurants. This isn't great, but it will have to do. I hope my ride is on time. I hate being late. That is one thing that always drove me crazy about my ex-wife. She was never on time. I tried hard to instill in MJ the value of promptness. He seems to have gotten it. Over the years, we spent so much time waiting for Melissa. I think he values punctuality as much as I do.

A lady entering the hotel interrupts my thoughts. She is hard not to notice. I watch her holding the door open for an elderly couple behind her. She smiles warmly at them, and I hear her exchanging pleasantries. In my line of work, I have been trained to observe and evaluate people. She strikes me as someone easy-going and confident. I notice her jean shorts and a great pair of legs before I notice her T-shirt with the service dog emblem. It suddenly dawns on me that she is my ride.

I quickly get up and approach her, extending my hand. "Mark Lancer," I say to her as we shake. I can see surprise in her eyes.

"Hi. Haley Duncan. I'm your ride. My car is the Honda right out front," she says with a smile.

As I follow her out, I find the cop in me assessing her. Thirty-five to forty would be my guess of her age. I would describe her as five feet four, around one hundred thirty pounds, brown shoulder-length hair, slender, athletic, maybe a dancer. A glance at her hand shows no wedding ring, but she strikes me as a woman who would be loved by someone. I would speculate that she is either divorced or in a long-term relationship.

"It will take about twenty minutes to get to the training site," she says as she starts the car. "If you have any questions, I might be able to answer them for you."

I can't help but ask, "So, did you pick the short straw to get stuck with transport duty?"

With a short chuckle, she answers, "No, I'm a puppy raiser and a volunteer for the program. You needed a ride, and I was more than happy to help out."

"Who picks me up?" I ask, wondering if I will be shuffled back and forth between drivers.

"I do. I'll be your only driver," she states.

"Won't this get in the way of your kids or your job?" I say, fishing for information.

"I'm on summer break right now, and although I'm not lucky enough to have children of my own, I anticipate having about one hundred thirty of them come September."

"You're a teacher?"

"Yes."

"Elementary?"

"High school English."

"Thanks for telling me that. I'll have to watch my grammar."

"Please, I'm sure you're a lost cause by now."

This catches me by surprise and makes me laugh. If she only knew how much I hate all the paperwork involved with my job. "I insist on paying for your gas," I tell her. "Is there some procedure I have to follow?"

Shaking her head, she quickly responds, "I volunteered to do this. I'm glad to be able to help out."

"I want to pay my way," I quickly respond.

"Let me remind you that the definition of a volunteer, which happens to be on my ninth-grade vocabulary list, is a person who offers to help or work without expecting payment or reward. So, no, you can't pay for gas, and I don't want to hear about this from you again."

I'll let the matter drop for now. I don't want to get off on the wrong foot with her. It could end up being a long two weeks. "So what's in this for you?" I ask.

"Excuse me?" She turns and shoots me a quick, bewildered look before turning her eyes back to the road.

"What do you get out of this?" I say again.

"Are you always so cynical?"

"Sorry, it's the cop in me."

Surprised, she asks, "You were a cop?"

Since the accident, this has been a sore spot for me. "I'm still a cop. State police, as a matter of fact." Not knowing what she knows about me, I add, "But since the accident, I'm no longer on the streets. I, like you, do some instructing, but mostly it's a lot of desk and lab work."

"You don't sound happy about that."

"I miss working the streets. I liked being around the people I served."

"Will you be able to do that type of work again?" she asks.

"The way I am now, I strongly doubt it!" I regret my tone immediately. "Sorry."

She doesn't say anything for a while, and I wonder how this conversation shifted to focus on me. I remind her, "You never answered my question."

"Oh yes, what's in it for me?" Although we are sitting at a light, she doesn't look at me and takes her time answering. "I feel good when I help others. I've seen what these service dogs can do for people, and I really like being a part of that." She pauses and then adds, "I also raised Jed, one of the dogs in your training."

This takes me by surprise, and I study her face intently.

"Here we are," she says as we pull up to the training center. "I will pick you up at four unless you finish early. Just text or give me a call. I wrote my cell number down for you in case there is a change in your schedule. I hope you have a wonderful first day." She turns and looks at me, note in hand. I am still intently searching her face. "Is something wrong?" she inquires.

As I take her note and get out of the car, I lean back in and say, "Thank you for raising Jed, my service dog."

CHAPTER 11

HALEY DUNCAN

What started out as an average morning has turned into an interesting day. I can't get the coincidence out of my mind that Jed is going to be Mark Lancer's dog. When I arrived at the hotel, Mark surprised me. Tall, dark, and handsome was not what I expected. I found him appealing and immediately wondered what his needs were that warranted a service dog. I can see him being a cop. He has the build and bearing for the job. I sensed a quiet guardedness about him and a manner that spoke of authority. I realize now that he suffers from seizures. The trainers informed me a couple of months ago that they were training Jed for this condition.

As four o'clock finally comes, I'm still trying to figure out if this is a conflict of interest. First, I need to talk to Mark about this issue. Then one of us needs to talk to the trainers. I wonder if this might be my last transport trip.

As I pull up to the building, I see Mark waiting at the entrance for me, notebook in hand. I take a quick glance at the time and see that I'm not late. That means training must have finished early today. I watch him as he walks to the car. His movements seem loose and easy, but I sense an alertness and readiness about him. He seems like the type of man who can make a woman feel safe. He's certainly the kind of man that would catch a woman's eye. I wonder why his wife or significant other is not here with him.

As he opens the door and settles himself inside, he sighs. "Do you believe it? I have homework."

I can't help smiling. "Homework is a good thing."

Grimacing as he flips through his notebook, he says, "Spoken like a true teacher."

"I am sure there is a lot for you to learn," I reply.

"I haven't done homework since college."

"I wish I could say the same."

Quickly looking up, I can see this surprises him. "What! Teachers give homework. They don't have to do homework."

"OK, here we go. Just who do you think grades all those essays, projects, and assignments the students do? And don't get me started on college recommendations, graduate courses, and other work the administration demands. I—"

With a chuckle, he cuts me off. "I surrender. Really, I have always admired teachers. We have a lot in common. In both our jobs, we have to deal with all types of people on a daily basis."

"The students are the best part of my job. I rarely have problems with them. I can't always say that about their parents," I add.

"I have dealt with some very interesting parents, too," he mentions, shaking his head in agreement.

"So, tell me how your first day went."

After settling back in the seat and stretching out his long legs, he replies, "Well, there are seven of us getting dogs. I guess we will get to know each other pretty well over the next two weeks. There are two autistic children, three veterans, a lady in a wheelchair, and me."

"Did you feel comfortable with the group?" I ask.

He looks out the window, then turns to me and says, "Honestly? No. Group work is not my strength. At lunch, I got to know the vets, so that made things easier." With a thoughtful look, he adds, "I never realized there would be so much to learn. I've been around police dogs and their handlers my whole career, and I never stopped to realize all the work that goes into their training. We didn't even get to see our dogs today!"

"You know, we really need to talk about Jed and the fact that I raised him," I say.

"What's the problem?"

I can feel him looking at me without even turning my head. Maybe I should have waited until I wasn't driving to bring this up. "Well, I will be driving you and Jed back and forth as your training progresses. Jed will recognize the car and me. It was a labor of love raising and working with him, but he had a lot of obstacles to overcome. I don't want to confuse him and get in the way of your bonding and training. Jed is a great dog now. The trainers invested a lot of work into him. I don't want to jeopardize this."

He reaches over and touches my arm. "Hey, relax. It'll be fine. If there are issues that develop, we'll deal with them as they come along," he says kindly but firmly.

"You seem so sure."

"I don't want you to worry about things that might not happen," he says with a calm, reassuring voice.

"You're using your police voice on me."

"Yes, I am. Is it working?"

"No. Promise me that you'll be honest with me and let me know if there are issues that bother you," I add, looking quickly at his face. "And promise me you will talk to the trainers about it tomorrow."

"Really, I think you are going overboard with this."

"Promise me," I insist.

"I take my promises very seriously," he says. I feel that about him, and I just wait for his reply. "OK, you got it."

"Thank you." I can feel the relief already as I pull up to the hotel.

"You're welcome. Thanks for the ride."

"Study hard."

I can see him shaking his head as he gets out of the car.

"Teachers," he mutters, half under his breath.

CHAPTER 12

MARK LANCER

This week has been exhausting. I forgot what it's like to be a student again. The trainers are teaching me the proper cues to use so that Jed understands me. We practice them all day long.

"Mark, walk with Jed over to that tree and then cue him to sit, lie down, and stay. Return back here and ask him to come," Cody says.

I keep a close watch on Jed to make sure he heels properly as we walk to the tree. He sits, goes down, and stays, all the time watching me intently. When I cue, "Come," he gets up quickly and runs over to me for his treat.

The trainers seem to be pleased with the way Jed and I are working together. Even though we've only been together a few days, I feel a real connection to this dog. He makes me proud when he quickly performs the cues I give him, and he makes me laugh with some of his antics and expressions. Just thinking of the way he tilts his head and looks up at me when we are practicing a long down/stay makes me chuckle. If he could talk, I can just imagine what he would be saying to me. *Really? How much longer? You are just sitting there. Not working. Not eating. Ball, a ball would be good here. Come on. Let's either work or play!*

Yesterday was the first night Jed was permitted to leave with me. It felt good to have him by my side. I didn't realize how lonely I've been in the evenings. Everyone we encountered had questions about Jed. I talked to more people last night than I have all week. It seems dog lovers are always ready to talk about dogs.

Haley's worry was for nothing. When we walked to her car for the first time, Jed was excited to see her, but he waited for my cue to say hello. He seemed familiar with the car and its smells, but after a few sniffs, he settled in nicely for the ride. Back at the hotel, he gave Haley a quick backward glance and then walked by my side to the door. That was that.

There is no training on weekends, so I guess Jed and I will do some exploring around town. He attracts attention everywhere we go. When people see his vest, they understand that he is working and leave us alone. Some understand the etiquette and ask permission to pet him. Most people smile as we pass by.

Haley is on time, as usual. I have to admit that I enjoy the rides. She is good company, and she exudes caring. I wonder how she spends her time and whom she spends it with. She never mentions anyone in our conversations. Then again, she has a way of always shifting the attention and conversation back to me. I really haven't learned much about her yet, which surprises me, because I'm usually the one asking the questions.

As we enter her car, I notice that her hair is in a ponytail, and she is wearing red shorts and a top. She looks so youthful that I wonder if I guessed her age wrong. And there's that smile again. Life must be good for her.

"Hi, Mark. Hi, Jed. You're halfway done now. Are you looking forward to the weekend?" she asks.

"Very much so. Right, Jed?" Looking back at him lounging in the back seat, I see him raising his eyebrows and giving me a questioning look.

"So, do you have weekend plans? Is anyone coming to visit you?" she asks.

"No plans, no visitors. I think Jed and I will do some exploring around town. Maybe find some new places to eat."

She listens to what I just said and seems to hesitate a bit. "Well, if you and Jed are interested, I thought I would make lasagna tomorrow night. If I don't have some help eating it, I will have leftovers for days. I was thinking you might be getting tired of restaurant food by now." She gives me a questioning glance.

I'm caught off guard by her invitation, but I immediately like the idea. "Aren't you getting tired of driving me around?"

She gives me an impatient look and says, "Is that a yes or a no?"

I think she knew all along that I would agree. "That would be a definite yes. Like Jed, I never turn down food."

"How about I pick you up around five o'clock? Bring Jed's food along. He can eat with Magic and Thunder."

"I take it Magic and Thunder are your dogs?"

"They're my two goldens. They helped me raise Jed. They miss him."

"Well, I guess I'm going to have to meet them then," I reply.

Now I'm thinking this weekend might not be so bad after all. I get a home-cooked meal, and I have the opportunity to learn more about Haley. Things are definitely looking up.

"Thanks for thinking of us. Jed and I will see you tomorrow," I say as we get out of the car.

"It's a plan. See you then," she remarks as she waves goodbye.

Later that evening, when Jed and I are settled in for the night, I think about her invitation. I wonder if there is a motive behind all that niceness. Looking over at Jed, I ask him.

"What do you think, Jed? Is she checking up on me? Does she want to make sure I'm the right owner for you?"

Jed stares at me, waiting.

"Come."

He continues to watch me as he walks over and puts his head on my knee. I pet him under his ears and down his back, enjoying the silkiness of his fur. A thought I haven't even considered comes to mind. What if I have a seizure while I'm at Haley's house? Maybe this isn't such a good idea after all . . . but what can it hurt? Even if I have a seizure, I probably won't see her again after next week. It dawns on me that I'll miss her company. I find her comfortable to be around, and I enjoy telling her about my day.

"OK, Jed, I admit it. I'm curious about her. So we'll go tomorrow, and I'll get my answers."

Chapter 13

Haley Duncan

I've been questioning myself all day. I'm so out of practice at this sort of thing. I keep telling myself, *This is not a date.* But cooking dinner for a man is something I haven't done in a long time. I like what I see in Mark. I feel a kinship with him and not just because of Jed. Life's battered him a bit, and this I can relate to. And he loves Jed. I can see it and feel it when I'm around them. I really just want to know this man better.

When I pick them up at the hotel, Mark leans over and gives me a bouquet of flowers as he gets in the car.

"For the cook," he says as he and Jed get situated.

"Oh, how kind of you. You shouldn't have," I say as I take in their scent. "But I'm glad you did." I feel myself smiling, and I start to relax a bit.

I notice that Mark is smiling back at me, and once again, I'm struck by how good-looking he is. He seems relaxed and more at ease than he has been all week. I wonder again about the women in his life. Wherever they are, I'm glad they aren't here. I feel fortunate to have him and Jed all to myself for the evening.

"I thought about bringing my dogs along for the ride, but I decided against it. They haven't seen Jed for a while, so there might be too much excitement," I explain. "So, have you been getting to know Homeland?"

"People are nice here," he says. "You can tell they are used to tourists. Although I think more people are talking to me because of Jed. They're curious about him and ask all kinds of questions. He sure does attract attention."

"I'm happy to see you working well together. The trainers have good instincts when matching dogs, but there are no guarantees. They got it right with you and Jed. The two of you seem to make a great team."

"Was it hard for you to give him up after all the time you put into him?" Mark asks, looking intently at me. "And don't give me the standard answer about changing a life that I have been hearing all week," he adds.

I let out a little sigh before responding. "OK, it hurts, but I always knew he wasn't mine, that I was doing this for someone else. I'm glad it's you. Fate somehow arranged it so I've been able to get to know you. That makes it a lot easier for me."

As I pull into my driveway, I notice Mark checking out my home. "So this is where Jed spent his puppyhood."

"Come in and meet his buddies," I say. Jed's tail is wagging furiously as he waits beside Mark while I unlock the front door.

"Meet Magic and Thunder. They're the ones who really mentored Jed. Magic is the smaller of the two. She can look at you with those big, brown eyes, and all your troubles can disappear like magic. Thunder is the elder. He's my big boy." I explain this as I lead the dogs to the backyard, where they can properly greet each other.

"This is nice. You have it all fenced in. They have room to run," Mark remarks as he checks out the backyard.

"Fencing makes life a lot easier, especially mornings and evenings. What do you call home?" I ask.

"Condo. It's close to everything, and I have all I need on one floor." He pauses for a moment, and he seems lost in thought. "But now that I have Jed, I might have to rethink it."

"Well, Jed is very adaptable. You are his life now."

"You and the trainers did a great job with him. You seem to have done a good job with your own dogs, too," Mark comments after noticing how the dogs sat when we entered the house and waited for me to tell them they could visit.

"Well, my husband was here to help with Magic and Thunder," I say.

"Ex-husband?" he asks.

"Deceased. He died almost four years ago now. It was cancer." I pause and shake my head. "It was awful."

Mark remains silent, then asks, "How long were you married?"

"Sixteen years."

"I'll bet you were good at it," he says, looking over at me.

That makes me smile. He surprises me at times with his reflections on things. "I loved being married. It was the happiest time of my life."

Shaking my head to clear those thoughts away, I change the direction of the conversation. "As you can see"—I gesture to the patio table I have set—"I thought we would eat outside. It should be a beautiful evening. I have some things to do in the kitchen. Do you want to come in or stay out?"

"I think I'll watch the dogs play some more," Mark says.

"They are a sight, aren't they?" I turn and watch as the three dogs continue their romp. "They live in the moment. It's such a good lesson for all of us," I add as I start back into the house.

I don't have much to do since I made the lasagna this afternoon. As I begin to prepare the salad, I watch Mark from the kitchen window. He's left the deck and is now out throwing the tennis balls for the dogs. My breath catches as I see him letting loose with them. He stops, juggles the tennis balls, and ends up tossing them in different directions. I can see him tilting his head back and laughing as the dogs scatter and chase each other. It makes me laugh too. Mark seems like a good man. I find myself drawn to him. Again, I wonder about the women in his life and why they're not here right now.

As I join them outside, Mark asks, "Is it hard to take care of the house and the yard by yourself? Do you have help?"

"I manage. I have a riding lawn mower. That makes mowing the easiest work I do. I also have wonderful neighbors who look out for me. They seem to get great pleasure out of doing random acts of kindness without telling me."

"It must keep you busy."

"About a year after Jack died, everyone started hounding me to sell the house and buy a condo. Everyone kept asking why I would want such a big place by myself. It was easy to dismiss them. Why would I leave? I love it here. It's set up perfectly for the dogs. All my memories are here. This is home. That seemed to take care of it."

He doesn't respond to this, and I can see he is lost in thought. As we both watch the dogs, I ask, "What is Jed's new home like?"

"Well, I've lived in a condo since the accident." He pauses, watching the dogs. "It just made life easier. But being here and seeing how you live makes me long for a house and some land again. Now that I have Jed, I might have to rethink some things."

"So you didn't always have seizures?" I ask. This is something I've been wondering about since I met him.

"No. They developed from the accident."

I wait, hoping for more.

As he continues to watch the dogs play, he tells me what happened. I get the feeling he doesn't share this very often.

"It was a routine traffic stop. The car pulled off right next to the guardrails because there was no berm. I went to the driver's window and asked for his information. The next thing I knew, I was flying through the air, and I woke up in the hospital. It was just my luck that an eighty-year-old man driving by lost control of his car and crashed right into me. Later they found out he suffered a heart attack. Everyone survived, but my injuries were the worst. The broken bones healed easily enough, but the brain trauma caused the seizures. The doctors have been trying to control them ever since."

I touch his arm and look into his eyes. "I'm sorry that happened to you. As my kids at school say, life sucks at times."

He lets out a small sound. "That's what my son says too."

"You have a son?" I ask.

"MJ. He's in his first year of med school on the West Coast. Great kid. I don't deserve him. It was his idea for me to get a service dog. He hounded me until I finally signed up. I don't know how he became so wise."

"And your wife?" I ask.

"Divorced. Five years now. MJ left for college, and she packed up and moved to California."

I wasn't going to let it go at that, so I just waited. He looks over at me and then continues.

"We married right out of college, and she got pregnant right away. At first, she was busy with MJ and didn't have time to realize that she didn't like being a cop's wife. It didn't take long for me to see that she was unhappy with our life. I tried. I really did. Even when the complaints intensified, I was always optimistic that things would get better."

Watching him closely, I can read the frustration on his face as he shakes his head.

"But there was no making her happy. Looking back, I can see that she was just biding her time. I do give her credit for sticking it out till MJ left."

He pauses, runs his hand through his hair, and looks downward. It looks like he is debating with himself whether to say more.

"Now I can see that Melissa was a bad choice for me. You know what they say. With age comes wisdom. I don't plan on going down that road again," he adds.

"Do you mean marry again?" I ask.

"I will never marry again," he says.

"Well, if there is one thing I've learned, it's to never say never. Life is full of surprises and second chances," I say.

He looks at me with skepticism. "Would you marry again?"

"In a heartbeat," I quickly respond, surprised by my own answer. "But it would take the right man."

"I would think you would have no trouble with that," he says.

I can see him sizing me up as men do. I shake my head with a smile and look at him. "You are a very kind man." I turn and head for the door. "I need to do some things in the kitchen. We'll be ready to eat soon."

While I finish the preparations, I think about the conversation and the things he revealed. I wonder about his ex-wife and his son. I always feel sad when I hear the stories of divorce. Jack and I had tough times, too, especially with my infertility, but the one constant in our lives was the love and respect we had for each other. We were both good with commitments. I was blessed for sixteen years. I wonder if it can happen again to me.

I yell outside, "Thunder! Magic! Food!" The dogs race inside for mealtime. I see that Jed started to come with them but then turned to Mark for his cue. I'm losing him, I think to myself. This is a good thing.

Mark comes in and finds a corner to feed Jed. Once the dogs have eaten and are settled, we head out to the deck for our dinner.

"This lasagna is very good," Mark says.

"How long has it been since you had a home-cooked meal?" I ask.

"I can't even remember," he responds.

A pleasant quietness follows as we both enjoy the food.

"Did the trainers explain to you where Jed got his name?" I ask after a while.

"No, do you know?"

"Yes. It was one of the first things I asked when I got him. I learned that every litter they breed has a theme. The themes can come from the trainers, organizations, or people. The organizations or people can donate money and then choose the theme of the litter and the name of the puppies."

"That's a great way to raise money," Mark comments.

"Or memorialize someone or something," I add.

"That too."

"Jed came from the Beverly Hillbillies litter. Do you remember that old TV show? After all these years, it still makes me laugh when I watch the reruns. Anyway, there were five puppies in Jed's litter. The two blacks were named Jed and Jethro, the two blonds were Elly and Pearl, and the one chocolate was Duke."

"I never would have guessed," he chuckles.

"I always ask. It never ceases to amaze me how they come up with their ideas," I add.

"So, if you had the chance, what would you name a litter?" Mark asks.

"Gee . . . as I would say to my students, good question . . . I would probably go with classic writers. Poe, Kipling, Whitman, London, Hugo, Twain for males, and Stowe, Dickenson—no, that is too much of a mouthful—Woolf, Alcott, not sure about that one either, and Austen for females." I stop and change directions. "Or a punctuation litter might be fun. Comma, Period, Adverb, Colon, Dash, Slash, Hyphen." I let those sink in before saying, "OK, your turn. Give me a police litter."

"Hmm . . . that takes some thought." I can see him gazing off. "OK, here goes. How about Arrest, Sting, Case, Rap, Bail, Line-up, Miranda, Priors, and Sergeant?"

"That was good."

"You know cars would make a good litter name," he adds. "Chevy, Kia, Ford, Mercury, Honda."

I jump right in with "Audi, Lexus, Lincoln, Mercedes." Pausing for a moment, I add, "You know, we're really good at this. I will have to suggest to the trainers that we would make wonderful consultants if they ever run out of ideas."

By this time, we are both done eating, and we start to bring the dishes back into the kitchen. "How about we take a walk around the neighborhood with the dogs before dessert?"

"Sounds good to me," he says.

It is a beautiful August evening, and we are surrounded by the colors of late summer as we walk.

"I am blessed to have great neighbors who are so helpful to me. Steve and Faith live in this house. He's always doing something in the yard. I'm surprised he's not out now."

A few houses down, Mark points to a beautiful red maple tree. "I used to have one like that in the front yard of my old house. I like your neighborhood," Mark says. "There is land between the houses, and you can walk the streets without worrying about traffic."

"I've always been happy here," I reply. As I look over at Mark and Jed, I can see that they make a remarkable team. It gives me great satisfaction to know that I played an integral part in their partnership. I wonder about his seizures, but I don't ask.

It is dusk as we return to the house. "Would you like to see some movies I took of Jed while we have dessert?"

"I would like that," he replies.

I put out the cookies, brownies, ice cream, and toppings, and we both help ourselves.

"Now, this is my kind of dessert," he says.

"I can't imagine life without ice cream," I add. With bowls and drinks in hand, we head to the family room. "Now, if my technology works as it should, you can see Jed grow up before your eyes."

We spend the next half hour laughing and watching clips of Jed at home, in public, and at training sessions. It is bittersweet for me to see these movies again. As I watch, I'm surprised that I feel myself tearing up. Jed always had a way of tugging at my heartstrings.

When we are done, Mark asks, "Could you make a copy of this for me?"

"I can do that. I can give it to you before you leave. I should have thought of it before."

"I could never do that," Mark says. "Technology is not my strong point. MJ always takes care of those kinds of things for me."

"I'm certainly no expert, but we continually get training at school, which is very helpful," I say.

As I get up, he picks up his dish and heads with me to the kitchen. "It's almost ten o'clock. You should think about taking us back to the hotel."

"OK. How about taking some goodies back with you? It will keep you sweet," I tease.

"I never pass up food, thanks." He smiles.

After bagging some leftovers for him, we pile the three dogs into the car and head out. It is a quiet ride. I find myself wishing that the evening wasn't ending. I glance over at Mark and see he is looking out the window. I wonder what he's thinking. I can't help but wonder how he sees me.

As we pull up at the hotel, he touches my arm. I turn to face him, and he says, "Thank you for tonight. I can't remember when I had such a wonderful evening."

"Me, too," I add.

He leans over and, to my surprise and delight, gives me a quick kiss on the cheek. He gets Jed and turns to say, "You are an amazing woman. I'm lucky that I got to know you."

As I watch him walk with Jed into the hotel, shaking my head, I say to myself, "No, I'm the lucky one."

CHAPTER 14

MARK LANCER

This is my last drop-off. I look over at Haley, and then I glance back at Jed. It is a quiet ride back to my hotel. When we arrive, we all get out of the car. She gives Jed a hug, and I can hear her whisper into his fur, "I'm so proud of you. Take good care of Mark." She gets up, and with a sad smile, she turns to me and says, "You take good care of Jed, and he will take good care of you."

"I will," I reply.

She quickly turns away from me, and I can see her struggling with her emotions. Before she is able to get back in the car, I hand her my card with my email, home address, and phone on it.

"So you can stay in touch," I tell her.

Looking down at it, she replies, "Thank you."

"No, thank you," I say as I grab her hand and wrap my arms around her. It feels right to have her there in my arms. Neither one of us seems to want to let go. Haley pushes away first, gives me a sad smile, and gets in her car. Jed and I stay there and watch her until she drives out of sight.

Since the accident, I've felt like my life has been on hold. I was waiting and hoping to get my old life back. All the doctors had to do was find the right medications. But getting Jed, meeting Haley, and going through this training have made me realize a few things. I don't want my old life back. I want to create a whole new one with Jed by my side.

Haley has not been far from my thoughts since the moment I met her. She might think that she saw the last of us today, but I have other plans. I know she'll be getting in touch with me again, and I'm looking forward to seeing how this all plays out.

"I appreciate you driving me home, Cody."

"My pleasure," he answers with a grin. "What's not to like? I get free food and lodging with you for the next three days, and I get a free tour of Pittsburgh. I've never been there."

"And you hope to catch me having another seizure," I say.

"That's the plan. I hope you can oblige me," he replies.

"The one I had at team training wasn't enough for you?"

"It was the first day. I didn't even have Jed there yet."

"The next day, some of the other clients thanked me for getting them dismissed early."

"That doesn't surprise me. The first day is always a grind."

"Do you think Jed will be able to alert me when one is coming?"

"Jed's smart, but it will take time. He has to get to know you and figure it out. I hope to help with that if I witness a seizure in the next few days."

I'm curious about Cody and the job he does. I don't know if it's the cop in me, but I always like to get background information on people if I can.

"I see you're wearing a ring. Your wife doesn't mind you being away for the next few days?" I ask.

"Erin, my wife, is traveling for work this weekend, so it really timed out perfectly," Cody says.

"What kind of work does your wife do?"

"She's a lawyer. Lucky for me, she makes the big bucks. That way, I can have this job that I love."

"Pay isn't great, huh?" I ask.

"Well, my pay wouldn't allow us to live in the new home we just bought. Most of the funding for the Homeland Service Dog Association comes from grants and donations. Thank goodness, there are a lot of generous people out there who love animals and know the impact they can make on people's lives."

"How did you become a trainer? Did you go to school for it?"

"Not really. I've always loved animals. When I was growing up, we had all types of critters around the house. My mom was a volunteer puppy sitter for the association. That meant that we watched a lot of different puppies when their raisers were not available."

I see him smiling, and I right away know it was a good childhood.

"Nice way to grow up," I say.

"The best," he answers. "I've worked with animals most of my life. When it came to a career path, studying animal husbandry in college was a no-brainer. My plans were to spend my life around animals. So far, it's working out well."

We both get quiet after this exchange. With a four-hour car ride ahead of us, Cody and I do a little more talking but pass the rest of the time listening to oldies on the radio. I'm glad for the downtime. These last two weeks have been a whirlwind of activity. I have a lot to think about and many plans to make.

I glance back at Jed lounging in the back seat, and a sense of protectiveness comes over me, something I haven't felt in a long time. I feel myself smiling when I look at him, and I realize that I feel more like myself than I have since the accident. As those big brown eyes look up at me, I silently speak to him. *Jed, I promise you, I will give you a good life. From here on out, we're in this together.*

I want Jed to have a place like Haley's. A place where he can run and smell and just be a dog. I want a house again, smaller this time, with some land and a fenced-in yard. Some place that Jed and I can call home.

Chapter 15

Haley Duncan

Locking up my classroom and heading down the empty hallway, I realize my life has returned to its normal routines. The start of this new school year helps fill up the emptiness I have felt since Jed and Mark left. September is always a busy time filled with high hopes, new plans, and great expectations. I'm fully immersed in trying to learn about my students and all the new initiatives set up by the school. But there is an emptiness that I carry around with me. I make sure no one sees it, but I know it's there. I remind myself that every ending is also a new beginning. I know that in time things will get better, but right now, it hurts.

Before getting in my car for the drive home, I check my phone. It's been a month now since Mark and Jed left. I haven't heard anything from him. I had hoped that he would text or email to let me know how things are going. I know I could have contacted him. After all, he gave me his card, but it just didn't seem the right thing to do.

Pulling out of the parking lot, I leave all school thoughts behind me and focus on Mark and Jed. I happened to see Cody while I was volunteering last week, and I couldn't help myself. "So, how did everything go with Mark and Jed during your visit?"

"Good. My stay went well," he replied.

"How is Jed doing?" I inquired.

"You know Jed. He doesn't skip a beat. He is adjusting beautifully to his new environment and to Mark's needs."

"I'm glad to hear that."

"You should be proud of the work you did with Jed. He is definitely working well for Mark. Take some time now for yourself and then give some thought to raising another puppy for us," Cody said.

Time is definitely what I'm taking. Not only do my dogs and I miss Jed, but I miss Mark too. For the first time since Jack died, I met someone to whom I'm attracted. As I gather my schoolbag and get out of the car, I think, *Really, Haley? You find a man that lives four hours away? And to make matters worse, he can't drive. His life is there, and yours is here. Of all you know, he might have someone special back there. So quit thinking about him.*

It is late afternoon, and I'm outside grading some essays when the dogs start to go crazy. I walk around to the front of the house and see that the UPS truck is stopped there.

"Hello, are you sure you have the right house?" I ask.

"I do if you are Haley Duncan," he says.

"That's me, but I'm pretty sure I didn't order anything."

After signing, he hands me a small box and gets back in his truck. The box is pint size and barely weighs anything. I move it from hand to hand as I return to the backyard. Putting my grading aside, I place the box on the table and notice there is no return address.

"Hmm," I mutter to myself. "I hope this is safe."

I open the box, and there is a smaller gift-wrapped square box inside. After carefully unwrapping the paper and moving aside the tissue, I find a beautiful bracelet. It looks to be an original piece and maybe crafted by an artist. I pick it up and feel the smoothness of the two intertwined strands of silver. There is an engraving on the inside of each strand.

One strand reads:

To always keep me near —Jed

The other strand reads:

Thank you for Jed —Mark

I start to tear up as I look at Mark's gift. I am overcome with its beauty and the meaning it bears. His thoughtfulness touches my heart. I slip on the bracelet beside the yellow cancer band that I wear in Jack's memory. As I brush the silver strands with my fingertips, I feel connected to Mark and Jed, and I wonder if that's what Mark intended. I notice that there is a small card addressed to me in Mark's handwriting at the bottom of the box. I unfold it and read.

Haley,

I wanted to give you something as a thank you for everything that you've done for me. I noticed that you always wear the yellow cancer band, so I thought you might like this. I hope I'm right.

This is a thank you for all the rides back and forth to training. You started and ended my days on a positive note. I really enjoyed your company.

This is a thank you for dinner. You reminded me what a real home feels like.

This is a thank you for Jed. I can't tell you how important he is to me and how different my life has become.

Mark

I make the call. I programmed his information in as soon as he gave me his card. While it rings, I search for the right words to say to him. As an English teacher, this should be easy for me, but I find I'm at a loss.

CHAPTER 16

MARK LANCER

Discreetly checking my phone during the meeting, I see that the call is from Haley. Damn, bad timing—I can't answer it now. I'm in the middle of an important briefing about this undercover arms case we're working on, so I have to let the call go to my voice mail. I wasn't sure how or when Haley would contact me, but after sending her the bracelet, I knew it was coming. It isn't until the evening that she calls again.

"Mark, it's Haley. I love the bracelet. It's perfect."

"I'm glad. I had it made for you."

"I can tell."

"I hope you'll wear it."

"I doubt I'll take it off."

"Good."

"It was such a surprise. Wearing it makes me feel closer to you and Jed."

"I'm glad. How's your new school year going?"

"It's going well. I got my students settled in, and I am back to all my grading. You'll appreciate this. I had my seniors write about something that changed their lives. Those are the papers I'm grading now."

"Gee, I wonder where you got that idea."

"The essays are amazing. My students really seemed to get into the assignment. These are a joy to grade." She pauses and then asks, "How are you and Jed?"

"Very well. I don't seem to be having as many seizures since I got Jed."

"Mark, that's wonderful."

"It's been good because I've been busy. I put my condo on the market, and it sold in a week. Luckily, I found a nice little house with a yard in a location that should be perfect. I settle at the end of the month."

"Wow, you have been busy. Do you have a lot to move?"

"No, when I moved into the condo, I had to get rid of a lot of stuff from the house. I don't even need a moving company. Greg Dobler, my old partner, and some of my other cop friends are going to help me."

"I am so happy for you and Jed."

"You know, once we get settled, you and Magic and Thunder are invited out to see Jed's new home."

"I would like that."

"I would like that too."

"Can you keep me posted on how things are going with the two of you?"

"My pleasure."

"Mark, thank you again for the bracelet."

"Enough said. Go back to your grading."

"I could have some trouble concentrating."

"Just give them all As."

"They would like that."

After saying goodbye, I find myself smiling and thinking about how well the conversation went. I look down at Jed and ask him the question that is floating around in my mind. "I wonder if she will really come or if she was just being nice."

Chapter 17

Emails

From: Mark Lancer
To: Haley Duncan
Subject: Update
Haley,
It was nice talking to you the other day. I hope you got all your grading done. Please excuse all my grammar and spelling mistakes. I wasn't lucky enough to have an English teacher like you when I was growing up. Jed and I are doing well. In fact, I'm taking a break from packing. Jed has been giving me a "yes" or "no" about what I should keep and what I should discard. Closing is Monday on the condo and Tuesday on my new place. I'm glad things are moving quickly. I'm ready to go. Jed needs room to run and a place to be just a dog. I have the fence guys ready for installation after closing. Moving is set up for this weekend. By next week, I will be unpacking all the boxes that I am now packing. It's a lot easier going from a condo to a house rather than the other way around. Hope all is well with you, Magic, and Thunder.
Mark

From: Haley Duncan
To: Mark Lancer
Subject: Hi
Hi Mark and Jed,
Wow! Things are really progressing. Thanks for the update. You will find Jed very adaptable to any new surroundings. As long as he's with you, he's home. I have been thinking about the two of you. I hope everything went smoothly with your closing, and I hope all goes well with your move this weekend.
Haley

From: Mark Lancer
To: Haley Duncan
Subject: All moved in
Haley,
I wanted to wait until I was all moved in and my computer was set up to email you. Jed and I could not be happier in our new home. I realize how much I've missed having a yard and more space to putter around in. Jed has claimed the backyard as his own. When we go out there, he goes on patrol, checking every nook and cranny. He is fun to watch when he's working and when he's just being a dog. If you are ever in our neck of the woods, you need to come and check us out. I have room for guests with dogs, and I am master of the grill. I also could use a female's advice on some decorating issues. I want to make this house into a real home for Jed and me. Please think about it.
I hope school is going well. Keep those teenagers in line.
Mark

From: Haley Duncan
To: Mark Lancer
Subject: OK, I can't help myself.
Hi Mark and Jed,
I am finding it hard not to take you up on your offer. If you are not busy next Saturday, the dogs and I are up for a road trip. If we leave at about eight, we could get there around noon. If the dogs need a rest stop, it will take longer. We can leave after dinner and still get home at a reasonable hour. Let me know if this works for you.
Haley

_____

From: Mark Lancer
To: Haley Duncan
Subject: It works.
Haley,
Excellent. My new street address is 5 Hummingbird Lane. Jed and I are looking forward to seeing all three of you next Saturday.
Mark

CHAPTER 18

HALEY DUNCAN

Filled gas tank—check. Finally decided on outfit—check. Packed Magic and Thunder's food—check. Car packed—check.

It is bright and early, and we are on our way to Pittsburgh. I keep asking myself what I'm doing. I feel like one of my students who just got asked to the prom. I couldn't wait for today to arrive, and now that it's here, I find my emotions playing havoc with me. I keep telling myself to relax or this is going to be a long four hours of driving.

I always find beginnings exciting, and I wonder how this day will unfold. I feel that Mark's interested in me. Even though I'm out of practice, I can sense it like any woman can. I still find it hard to believe that he doesn't have a girlfriend in his life. He could attract any number of women if he wanted. Women would find a man like him irresistible. Plus, Jed brings all kinds of attention to him. They make a hard-to-resist pair.

It's been a long time since I've been attracted to a man. Mark is the first man I've looked at with interest since Jack died. I think Jack would have liked Mark. Although we never talked about it, I believe Jack would not want me to be alone.

I hit the music button on my phone and let the sound drown out my thoughts. It is programmed to play my favorite songs from the music file. I love having the ability to decide on my own playlists. Every song in my favorites folder has a special meaning for me. Listening to them evokes memories of different periods of my life. "Under the Boardwalk" by The Drifters just finished playing. Every time I hear it, I think of vacations at the shore. My parents took Cassie and me there every summer when we were growing up. Elvis's "Can't Help Falling in Love" is playing now. This one is a bittersweet memory because it was the first song Jack and I danced to at our wedding. I sing along with the songs as I drive. Thank goodness it is only Magic and Thunder in the car with me. As the hours pass, I think about the day ahead. It is a long drive, and this might be my first and last visit.

As I near his street, I notice the bus stop at the corner. I'm sure that was a big selling point for him. Hummingbird Lane is a circle of eight homes, and his house is located at the end of the street.

It is a two-story building with gray siding and stone accents. A porch runs the length of the front, and I see Mark and Jed waiting there for us. As I pull into his driveway, I can actually feel my heart beating. It's funny that even at my age, I can feel the same kind of excitement I felt back in my teens.

I watch Mark and Jed start down the porch steps to greet us. Mark is wearing jeans with a blue shirt. I forget how ruggedly handsome he is.

"Welcome to our new home," Mark exclaims as I get out of the car. "Did you have any trouble finding us?" Before I can get any words out, he embraces me with a quick hug. "It's nice to see you again," he says as we move apart. I can see Jed's tail wagging furiously. He is having trouble containing himself with all the excitement of seeing the three of us again.

I am surprised and pleased by Mark's greeting. "Mark, the house looks great. Let me get the dogs out, and you can show me around."

"Let's go around back first and let the dogs get reacquainted. I'm sure Magic and Thunder can't wait to get moving after four hours in the car. How was the drive?" he inquires.

"It was fine. There was very little traffic, and I managed not to get lost. The dogs mostly slept, so I didn't even have to make any stops."

He takes my hand and looks at the bracelet shining in the sunlight. "I knew it would look good on you," he says.

"I haven't taken it off since I got it," I respond.

He keeps hold of my hand and leads me to the side yard where his fencing starts. The black iron fence he has added blends perfectly with the house. The backyard is large and backs up to a grove of trees. My hand feels lost when he lets go to unfasten the gate.

"Wow! This is dog heaven back here," I exclaim as I move into the yard. "How much land do you have?"

"It's a little under an acre," he replies.

"It's wonderful!"

"It is, isn't it?" he replies modestly. "Come on. Let me show you the house. We can let the dogs outside. When they want to join us, Jed can show them the dog door."

"You've thought of everything."

"I've learned some things from my visit to your house."

As he leads the way to the deck, I notice that the back of the house is made up mostly of windows.

"I bet you get some great views of the woods and surrounding fields from those windows."

"It was a big selling point for me," he says. We head inside through the back door, which opens up into the kitchen. "Kitchen and family room combination."

Smiling, I ask, "Is it always this neat?"

"I like things to have order," he replies with a sheepish smile. As we enter the living room, he says, "As you can see, I need some more furniture."

"I love the fireplace and the high ceiling. I can see you and Jed sitting here on a winter night." I notice a picture of a handsome young man on the mantle. I walk over to study it more closely.

"That's MJ," he informs me.

"Of course it is. He looks a lot like you," I reply, marveling at the resemblance.

"He's a great kid. Luckily he ended up with the best parts of his mother and me." He turns, and I follow him up the stairs. "Three bedrooms—well, really two bedrooms and an empty room right now. I hope MJ will use his sometime," he says.

"I'm sure he will, and you will have to get that empty room ready in case he brings home a friend," I add.

"Maybe this afternoon you can give me some advice on that and some other things I need," he remarks.

"I can do that, and you can show me around your town at the same time."

"Sounds good."

His bedroom suits him. All the furniture is dark brown, and a king-sized bed dominates the room. I notice the walls are bare of pictures. "So, where does Jed sleep?" I ask.

"I swore he was not getting on the bed. That lasted about a week. Now he has his side, and I have mine," he answers, shaking his head.

"I understand completely," I say, smiling up at him.

We head downstairs, and he shows me the finished basement. I stop to look at his framed certificates and awards. "You are very accomplished."

"I *was* very accomplished," he states.

"I am sure you are still doing meaningful work," I say, watching him. He straightens one of the frames before shaking his head and looking at me.

"It's not the same. I like some of the work I do, but it is still hard for me to watch my fellow troopers go out on patrol while I stay back at the station and work behind the scenes," he says.

I can hear the regret in his voice. "I know that feeling. I still can't look at a baby without feeling a huge sense of loss." I pause, then add, "Life just isn't fair."

Mark looks at me. "You got that right. I guess I should feel lucky that they didn't give me early retirement. Even with these seizures, I'm still a help to them. Come on. Let's grab some lunch. I bought hoagies for us."

The dogs join us as we enter the kitchen.

"Can I help?" I ask.

"Grab whatever you want to drink from the fridge. You can get me an iced tea. Then just relax. I got this."

I sit down at the kitchen table and take turns petting the three dogs as he gets everything ready. Lunch is pleasant. We both talk about our work and the antics of our dogs. Sitting with him in his kitchen seems so comfortable to me and so right.

The afternoon proves to be just as enjoyable. We load the dogs in my car, and I drive as he shows me the area. I see the station where he works and the places he shops. We stop at some stores and look at a variety of furniture pieces. He has a pretty good sense of what he likes and dislikes, but he listens carefully to my suggestions. Although he doesn't purchase anything, he says he has a lot to think about. It is revealing for me to observe him in his own environment. I'm sure at work he has to make quick decisions, but I can see it's more his nature to explore all the possibilities before making a choice.

By the time we arrive back at his house, the afternoon is gone. After he refuses my offers to help with supper, I give up and take the dogs out back. It's a joy to watch them frolic and play together again.

Mark calls out from the deck, "I hope you like steak. Maybe I should have asked you this before."

"I like steak, and the dogs love steak."

"Jed already taught me that. Let me guess, medium well?"

"Just medium if you can manage it."

"I'll try my best."

It is a little after six when we sit down to eat. The weather is still warm, so we eat outside on the deck. The dogs lounge under the table, eyeing us hopefully. The steaks are delicious, and Mark prepared salad and baked potatoes to complete the meal. We talk about the places we visited during the afternoon and what his plans are for the house. When we're done eating, I notice that he also left some small pieces of steak on his plate.

"It doesn't take these dogs long to train us, does it?" I say, smiling.

"I never thought I would see the day that I would be sharing my food with a dog," he says, shaking his head. "I know I'm not supposed to give Jed table scraps, but the first time I had steak, Jed rested his head on my foot and watched me the whole meal. When I didn't save him any, he lifted his head and let out this big sigh. He made me feel bad."

Knowing Jed, I could see him doing this, and it made me laugh. "That is so typical of Jed."

"Are you full, or did you save some room for dessert?" Mark asks. "There's a great ice cream place down the road."

Reluctantly I say, "I think we have to pass. It's already seven. The dogs and I should be thinking about starting home. The meal was delicious. Thank you." I look into his eyes and smile and say, "I have something for you in the car. Let me get it, and then I'll help you clean up."

"You are not helping me clean up. Jed and I have all evening to do that. Is it something from the Service Dog Association that you're getting?"

"No, this is from Magic, Thunder, and me. I'll be right back."

I go outside and remove the wrapped box I hid in the car. I have been planning this since I learned Mark was getting Jed. I was initially going to give it to him when he came for his required year-end testing, but with a new home, now seemed a better time. I'm anxious to see his reaction.

"What is this?" he asks when he sees the box.

"This is something for your new home. I hope you like it."

He takes the box, looks at it, then looks at me and says, "I like it already."

"Open it," I say impatiently.

"Are you using your teacher voice on me?" he asks.

I give him my "I am waiting" look I use on my students. He chuckles and unwraps the box and lifts out the picture. It is a watercolor of Mark and Jed from the back, walking together down a path that stretches off into the distance. Mark doesn't say anything right away. He just keeps looking at the picture. I anxiously search his face as I wait for some response. He finally looks at me, and I can see wonderment playing out on his face. "You made this for me?"

"Well, I took the picture of you and Jed that served as the basis for it. The design was my idea, but the art teacher at school was the one who painted it for you."

"It's the best gift you could have given me. Come here." He grabs my hand and enfolds me into his arms. "Thank you." I can feel him kiss the top of my head while he adds, "For everything."

I stay in his arms, savoring the feel of him. I could get used to being held by this man. I break away and look up at him. I can see he is moved by the gift. I smile at him and reluctantly say, "We have to go."

As I pick up the leashes, he grabs my hand and asks, "Will you come again?"

"I would like that," I answer him.

When I'm done putting the dogs in the car, I turn back around and face him. I can see Jed looking up at Mark. "We're staying, Jed," he says, and Jed seems to understand that Magic, Thunder, and I are the ones leaving.

"Thank you for coming this long way to see us, and thank you for the painting."

"I had fun. The dogs had fun. I'm glad you like the painting."

Mark looks at me as I look up at him. Placing his hands on the car on either side of me, he leans in and kisses me gently.

"I've wanted to do that all day," he says with a smile. "Have a safe trip back. Can you let me know that you get home safely?"

"I will," I say as I lower his head to mine and kiss him back. "That's so you know I've wanted to do that all day too." I smile up at him and turn and get in the car. He waves as I back out of the driveway. The last thing I see in my rearview mirror is Mark and Jed still standing there, watching us drive away.

The trip home seems like a blur. As the dogs snooze in the back, I spend the time reliving the day and thinking about Mark.

When I arrive home, I send him a text. *Home safe. Thank you for giving me a wonderful memory.*

He responds immediately. *Hope it is the first of many.*

CHAPTER 19

MARK LANCER

Jed and I watch Haley's car drive out of sight. As we enter the house, I can still feel her presence with me. I wander around to all the places she was. I can hear her voice in the empty rooms. I realize I like being with someone again. I like being with her.

Ever since I moved in, I've been imagining her here. When she finally arrived, I couldn't help but welcome her with a big hug. I saw that I surprised her, but she didn't hesitate to hug me back. She was wearing jeans and a soft green shirt and the bracelet I had made for her. She looked good.

Watching Jed play with Haley's dogs was a sight to see. They chased, jumped, and mouthed each other's ears with true delight. Although I noticed, even in his play, Jed was watchful of me. He ran back over to me for constant checks before racing back to Magic and Thunder. It made me wonder if he is lonely for canine companionship. That is something that I'll have to think about.

I enjoyed watching Haley's reactions to the house. I could tell she was pleasantly surprised. She was probably expecting some type of bachelor pad. As I scrub away at the grill, I think about the tragedies that Haley has faced. It is hard for me to envision how difficult her infertility must have been for her. I can't imagine my life without MJ. Even with a bad marriage and divorce, I wouldn't change a thing in my past because I have him. Haley had to battle her infertility, and then she had to watch her husband die. Shaking my head, I realize that her losses are greater than mine. This is humbling for me.

Done cleaning the grill, I lean on the deck railing and gaze out into the darkness of the woods. I feel a peacefulness settle over me as I continue to relive our time together. I found myself watching her throughout the day. I like her easy manner and the thoughtful way she expresses herself. She has a quick wit and an easy smile. I like how she makes me feel when she looks at me. I ask Jed, who is gazing up at me, "What on earth do you think she sees in me, Jed, a forty-five-year-old divorced man with seizures?" If only Jed could talk. I know he reads people better than I do.

As Jed and I head back into the house, I think about Haley leaving. Kissing her was in the back of my mind all day. I just couldn't let her leave without seeing which way this was going to go. Was she here for Jed, or was she here for me? When she kissed me back, I got my answer.

As I walk into the living room, I notice the painting on the coffee table. I pick it up and again admire the artistry of it. As I go to put it on the fireplace mantle beside MJ's picture, I notice that there is something written on the back of the painting. It says.

Mark,
With Jed, you will never walk alone.
Haley

Chapter 20

Haley Duncan

I finally find some time to call my sister. She knows I visited Mark and Jed over the weekend, and I'm sure she is curious about my trip.

"Hi, Cassie. How's it going there?"

"Crazy as always. All four of the kids are going in different directions. All I find myself doing is chauffeuring someone to basketball, soccer, gymnastics, or dance."

"Enjoy these days while you have them. This time in your life won't last long enough."

"I know. I hear you. Anyway, catch me up. I know you visited Jed last week. How is he doing?"

"Wonderful. He is working beautifully for Mark. They seem to have really bonded."

"Was it hard seeing him again?"

"Not really. We had a great visit. It was fun."

"But now it's final. You won't see Jed again. Isn't that painful saying goodbye all over again?"

"Well, that's not necessarily true."

"Not necessarily true. What does that mean?"

"Mark asked me to come back and visit again."

"Why? Is he having trouble with Jed?"

"No."

"Well?"

"All of us had such a good time. It was a joy to see the dogs together again."

"Haley, what's going on?"

"What do you mean, what's going on?"

"Yes, that's what I'm asking you," Cassie asks.

"I like him."

"You like him. What does that mean?"

"It means that I will visit again."

"Haley, he lives four hours away!"

"I know that, but a text, email, or call is less than a couple of seconds away."

"Is this why I haven't heard from you all week?"

"Mark's been calling me in the evenings."

"Why?"

"We like to catch up on what happened in each other's day."

"Haley, what are you getting yourself into?"

"Hopefully, a very nice relationship."

"Look, I'm sure he is a nice man, and I know how lonely you've been."

"No, you don't know how lonely I've been."

"OK, you're right. I've never lost a husband. I don't know how lonely you've been, but hear me out. He has seizures. He can't drive. He lives four hours away. How can this work?"

"Listen, Cassie. I don't need you to spell out the obvious. I don't know what will become of this, but I know how he makes me feel. I like feeling this way again."

"Are you falling in love with him?"

"No. I'm falling in like with him."

"I just don't see a future in this for you, and I don't want to see you hurt again."

"Cassie, I'm thirty-nine years old. I'm not a teenager anymore. I know how this works, and I'm willing to take the risk with him. He is a special man."

"Special man, huh? Well, he better realize how special you are."

"Please don't give me a hard time with this. He really makes me happy, and I haven't felt this way since before Jack's cancer."

"OK, but take it slow."

"Slow? We live four hours away. How much slower can we go?"

"You know what I mean. Oh darn, I have to cut this short. The kids are fighting over the computer again."

"OK. Listen. Don't worry about me so much. You have enough to handle. Say hello to everyone for me. I miss you guys."

"Same here. Take care and keep me in the loop about what's happening, all right?"

"Will do."

After I end the call, I take a moment to think about Cassie. I wonder if I would be as lonely if she lived closer. Then again, when I see her with her husband and four kids, it reminds me of everything I'm missing.

CHAPTER 21

MARK LANCER

I t's been a long time since I've done this. I think about it as I get rid of some of the dried needles that have fallen from the pine tree in front of my house. Home, it's not a house anymore. I'm beginning to feel at home.

"Well, hello," comes a female voice behind me.

As I turn, I find myself looking at a very attractive woman who looks like she just stepped out of a magazine. Every hair is in place. Her outfit is color-coordinated, with big pieces of jewelry around her neck and wrist. She is carrying a plate of something and has a smile on her face.

"Hello, can I help you?" I ask.

"Welcome to the neighborhood. I'm Alexandra Jennings. I live two houses up in the white colonial," she says, pointing to a big house up on the right. "I heard a man living alone bought this place."

"News must carry fast here. I just moved in."

"I'm a realtor. I'm up on all the land transactions. My son's been eyeing your dog ever since you moved in."

"That's Jed. He's friendly."

"I would have brought Brandon with me, but he's with his father this week. He's eight and a real animal lover. When he's home, I'm sure he'll love to meet Jed."

"No problem."

"Are you new to the area?"

"No, I've lived around here a long time. Just not here."

"You will find that most of the neighbors are friendly but keep pretty much to themselves."

"That sounds good to me."

"What's your line of work?"

"I'm a state policeman."

"Oh, that's great. I feel safer already. Not that this area isn't safe," she says with a smile.

When I don't respond, she hands me the plate. "Here, I hope you like chocolate chip cookies. This is my special recipe."

"Thank you, but you shouldn't have bothered."

"No problem. I like cooking for a man, and I don't have an opportunity to do it much anymore. Do you want to take a break and try one out?"

"I'll like to finish this now, but I'll certainly try one later."

"So you know your way around a kitchen?"

"I manage."

"Well, if you ever get tired of eating or cooking alone, let me know. I'm by myself a lot, and I don't know about you, but I hate to eat alone."

"I'll keep that in mind."

"You know where I live, so just drop off the dish anytime."

"Will do, and thanks again."

As I turn and head for the front door, thinking I've ended the conversation, she says, "You never told me your name."

"Mark Lancer."

"Well, Mark Lancer, if I can be of help in any way, just let me know."

Jed and I enter the house and head to the kitchen. Shaking my head, I look into Jed's eyes, "We need to watch out, Jed. Alexandra Jennings has 'available' written all over her."

"Hey, Dad, I'm glad you picked up," MJ says.

"MJ, it's good to hear your voice. It's been a while," I respond. "How are your classes and labs?"

"It's crazy here. It is harder than hard. I don't know how I can learn everything they want me to learn in the period of time they give me to learn it."

"I'm sure all the other first-year med students are saying the same thing."

"You are right there. Everyone is complaining. I consider myself lucky that I've made some good friends who are also good study partners."

"How's it going with Ed?" I ask.

"We only have one more week together. I wish Ed were alive so I could yell at him to take better care of his body. One look at his lungs, and you can see he was a heavy smoker and battling emphysema. It frustrates me every time I work on him. I just don't get how people can do that to themselves."

"Welcome to the real world, MJ."

"It still amazes me that people donate their bodies so we can dissect and study them. The anatomy books never quite prepare you for the real thing."

"Neither do the police manuals."

"I wish I knew Ed's real name and what his life was like."

"I felt the same way when I was working the streets."

"You still miss it, don't you?" he asks.

"Every day," I answer. There is a slight pause before I say, "Anyway, remember to stay organized and don't get bogged down by the big picture. Take everything in small steps."

"Spoken like a true detective."

"I wish."

"Dad, you know the behind-the-scenes work you do is just as important as the street work."

"I know. I didn't mean to sound like that."

"What are you working on now?"

"I helped crack a drug case last week, and I'm still working on that Internet scam I told you about. Mostly I've been spending time on that big undercover operation the station's been working on. It's been over a year now, and we've finally made some significant progress in infiltrating the organization. It's bigger than we ever imagined."

"Drugs?" he asks.

"No, weapons," I respond.

"At least I don't have to worry about you being safe."

"You got that right. I'll be the one back at the station writing up the reports. Anyway, I'm not complaining. Things are going well."

"You sound better. Is it Jed? How's he doing?"

"We're getting to know each other. You know, it's hard to believe, but since I got Jed, my number of seizures has decreased."

"That's great, Dad. Has he been able to alert you to the ones you do get?"

"It's a little too early to tell, MJ. I remember before my last seizure, he stopped and refused to move. He gave me this stare like I haven't seen from him before. I thought he needed to go out. When I woke from the seizure, he was lying almost on top of me. Next time he acts this way, I'm going to pay attention and lie down immediately. We'll see. He and I are a work in progress."

"That's good. How's the new house?"

"It's beginning to feel like home now. I should have done this years ago."

"Have you met any of the neighbors?"

"Just the lady two houses down, who came bearing cookies."

"Was she sizing up the new man in the neighborhood?"

"It certainly felt that way. I have to admit she is a nice-looking woman, but in the five minutes we talked, I found out she is divorced, has a son named Brandon who wants to meet Jed, loves to cook, and hates to eat alone."

"Sounds like an invitation to me."

"Me too. It's funny. When Haley asked me to dinner, I didn't get the impression that she was making herself available. I can't say that about Alexandra Jennings."

"Speaking of Haley, did she ever come for that visit?"

"Which time? She's come twice so far."

"Twice so far?"

"That's what I said. Is our connection bad? Are you having trouble hearing me?"

"No. I'm just wrapping my head around it."

"Around what?"

"What's going on, Dad?"

"What do you mean what's going on?"

"Now you're the one repeating yourself. What's her name again?"

"Haley Duncan."

"Doesn't she live something like four hours away?"

"Yes. Can you believe she and her dogs have made the trip twice already?"

"Did she come for you or Jed?"

"I hope for me, but I'm sure Jed figures into the equation."

"What did you do when she came?"

"First time, I showed her the house and town. Second time, we went up to the state park for the day. It was great. Her two goldens helped raise Jed, and the three dogs had a good time together. It was nice to see Jed just being a dog."

"I keep telling you, Dad—women will not be scared off by your seizures."

"I had one when I was with her in the park. All I remember is that Jed came running over to me. Next thing I knew, I woke up with my head on Haley's lap. It was a nice way to wake up."

"Is she why you seem happier?"

"I like her. I haven't felt this way in a long time."

"Will she come back?"

"She didn't seem the least bit fazed by my seizure. Since you can't come, I was thinking about asking her to join me for Thanksgiving. She's a teacher and will have time off over the holiday. Maybe she will stay for a couple of days."

"Go for it, Dad."

"We'll see."

"You deserve to be happy."

"I know, but so does she. Her life hasn't been easy either."

"Then you have a lot in common other than Jed."

"We'll see if she comes."

"If not, you can always ask Alexandra."

"I can see I'm going to regret telling you any of this."

"I'm rooting for you, one way or the other."

Hanging up the phone, I find that I'm glad MJ is so positive about me dating. He was not happy when his mother took up with a guy shortly after we separated. Although I've had plenty of opportunities over the years, I haven't been interested in any of the women who made themselves available. But from the first moment I saw Haley, there is something about her that captivated me. She's never far from my thoughts. I wonder if she feels the same.

I don't mind the bus ride to work and back. I have always been a big advocate of public transportation. I'm starting to recognize people and know when they get on and off. Jed and I usually try to claim the front seat across from the driver. Many of the regulars are starting to smile and greet us when they get on. The ride is only about fifteen minutes, depending on traffic, and it gives me time to unwind from work.

While Jed and I are walking from the bus stop to the house, there is a young boy playing catch with himself on the front lawn of a house on my street. As I get closer, he comes to the sidewalk and watches us.

"Hi," I say to him as we pass by.

"I like your dog," he replies.

I realize this is Alexandra's house, and this must be her son Brandon. He is wearing a jacket and baseball hat, and I have to smile at the small baseball glove on his left hand. He reminds me of MJ at that age.

"This is Jed. You may say hello if you like."

"Really, you mean I can pet him?"

"Yes. Sit, Jed. OK, go ahead, but always remember to ask before you pet a person's service dog."

I watch as he throws the glove and ball on the grass and pets Jed's head and his back.

"Hi, Jed. I'm Brandon. Can Jed do tricks?"

"I wouldn't call them tricks, but Jed is a working dog, so he understands many words. He just put in a full day on the job with me, so I'm not going to ask him to do anything."

"My mom said she met you."

"Yes, I enjoyed her cookies."

"She said you are the best thing to happen to the neighborhood in a long time. What does she mean by that?"

I've forgotten how open and honest children can be. "I think it's because I'm a state policeman," I say, not wanting to reveal the real reason behind his mother's words.

"Wow! Are you carrying a gun?"

"Not right now."

"Did you ever shoot anybody?"

"I try not to."

"Does Jed help you find the bad guys?"

"No. I had an accident a few years ago, and Jed just helps me if I need it." I happen to glance up and see the front door open, and Alexandra comes rushing out to join us. "Jed and I have to be going now. It was nice talking to you. Jed, home."

"Can I walk with you?" Brandon asks.

"Mark, hi, how have you been?" Alexandra says, a bit out of breath.

"Fine. We're just heading home."

"Mom, can I walk with Jed? You can see me from here."

"Well, if Mr. Lancer doesn't mind, we can both walk him home."

"I guess we're headed to the end of the circle then," I say, not seeing any way out of it.

"Brandon, did you introduce yourself to Mr. Lancer?"

"No, but I did to Jed." He turns and looks at me, extending his hand. "I'm Brandon Jennings."

"I'm Mark Lancer," I say, shaking his hand and making sure I don't squeeze his tiny fingers.

"That's Mr. Lancer to you, Brandon," his mother says.

"How about Officer Mark?" I say. I always used Officer Mark when I spoke to elementary schools. It seems to work well with children.

"Is there a Mrs. Officer Mark?" Brandon asks.

"No," I answer, glad that we are almost in front of the house. "Thanks for the company, and it was nice meeting you, Brandon."

"Tonight is taco night. Do you care to join us?" Alexandra asks.

"That would be awesome, and Jed could come too," Brandon exclaims.

"Sorry, I have plans for tonight. Thank you, though."

"Well, maybe Officer Mark will come another time," Alexandra says.

"Maybe," I add as I turn for the house. "Bye, Brandon, Alexandra," I say as I start up my walk.

"Bye, Jed. Bye, Officer Mark. Maybe I can walk you home tomorrow," Brandon says.

As I enter the house, I realize my evening plans have just changed. Instead of looking forward to a relaxing evening watching the ball game and talking to Haley, I now have to go out for dinner to keep myself honest. Brandon is a cute kid, and he's at a great age. I wouldn't mind spending some time with him. His mother is a different story. I know a lot of men would find her attractive. She exudes sex appeal, and she has the body to back it up. But now I find myself comparing every woman I meet to Haley. As innocent as dinner might be, it doesn't feel right to me. Somehow I feel it would be disloyal, and I don't want to do anything to jeopardize what I hope Haley and I might have together.

CHAPTER 22

HALEY DUNCAN

❝ Don't forget the bonus question on the board," I remind my students. "Remember, raise your hand if you have a question, and I will come to you. OK, get to work."

As I watch over my class, I realize I'm fighting distraction today. Thank goodness I'm testing and can get away with it. It's all because of Mark's phone call last night. We have been talking every evening since my last visit. I forgot how nice it is to share stories about the day's events with someone. He is starting to get a clear picture of a teacher's life while I am getting educated on the laws and the people who enforce them. He's a good listener, and I find myself opening up to him and sharing thoughts that I normally would keep to myself.

"So, do you have plans for Thanksgiving?" he asked me.

"Not really," I answered. "My parents are snowbirds in Florida, so I usually visit them over the Christmas holidays when I have more time off. I do have a standing invitation from Jack's family for all the holidays. They always make sure I know that I'm welcome to join them. Probably, though, I'll just stay home and meet up with some friends."

"Would you consider coming here and spending it with Jed and me?" he inquired. "I can easily take time off work, and we can make a little turkey and have our own Thanksgiving. Bring Magic and Thunder with you and stay at my house for as long as you want. I now have three bedrooms available." After a slight pause, he continued, "Mine being one of them. You can have your choice."

I was surprised by the invitation. "That is kind of you. Thank you for asking us."

Before I could say more, Mark added, "Don't answer right now. Just think about it. OK?"

The decision to go took no thought at all. There is nothing I would rather do than spend a couple of days with Mark instead of a couple of hours. The decision of where I want to sleep takes more thought. Keeping an eye on my students, I reminisce about my last visit.

"How do you feel about spending the day at the state park? The October colors are beautiful, and the weather is warm," Mark asked.

"That sounds like a great idea. The dogs will love it, too," I responded.

"I have a picnic lunch ready to go."

The park was about twenty minutes away. The reds, yellows, and oranges were so vibrant they looked like they'd been painted on the trees. We walked for a while, trying to find a secluded spot so we could let the dogs off leash and not bother anyone. As they investigated all the new sights and sounds, we picked a place to spread out the blanket. When Mark set the food bag down, Jed ran over to him.

"Do you smell the fo—"

Mark went down on one knee and then fell on his side. I rushed over to him. Jed was whining and pawing at his clothes. Mark was twitching slightly and then became still. I sat on the ground and cushioned his head in my lap. Jed rested his head and paws on Mark's chest. Unaware of what was happening, my two dogs continued their playing and exploring. Jed, Mark, and I remained this way for a number of minutes. When Mark opened his eyes, I could see him orientating himself to his surroundings.

"I was hoping you wouldn't have to witness one of these. Did I scare you?"

"Not a bit. I had a student a few years ago whose grand mal seizures always seemed to happen in my English class. This was nothing compared to those. Do you remember Jed getting all excited and running over to you? You thought he was trying to get at our sandwiches."

"Vaguely."

"I think he was trying to alert you."

"Cody told me to watch Jed for any behaviors out of the ordinary. That type of excitement might be a signal of an upcoming seizure. I'm going to have to pay more attention," he said as he started to get up.

"No, just stay put for a while. It's nice having you on my lap."

"I have to admit this is a great way to wake up from a seizure."

"Tell me about the accident and not just the highlights you give everyone else. Really tell me what it was like for you."

Mark took his time answering me. I didn't know if it was because of the seizure or if he was not used to talking about himself.

"When I woke up in the hospital, I didn't remember the accident. Everything seemed jumbled, and I was in a lot of pain. The doctors were concerned about my head injury more than the cracked ribs and dislocated shoulder. MJ was there, and I remember feeling bad that I was scaring him."

"I'm sure you were."

"I was able to reassure him enough that I got him to go back to college as soon as possible. Then I started the long, slow road to recovery."

"You were by yourself?"

"I preferred it that way. I hated feeling so helpless. Everyone was trying to do things for me, and I just pushed them away. I have always been independent, and I couldn't handle being dependent on other people."

"But it makes people feel good to be helpful."

"I was feeling so sorry for myself I didn't care what others felt. Then the seizures started, and the doctors had trouble controlling them. It was a very humbling time for me. I had trouble going from an able-bodied state policeman to a disabled one."

Running my fingers through his hair, I just waited.

"Once I recovered enough, Sergeant Dean, who heads our station, created a desk job for me. My partner, Greg Dobler, and some of the other troopers had to almost force me to get out of my house and get back to work. Every day was a struggle for me. I was angry with everybody and everything, especially my doctors. I couldn't believe that in this day and age, modern medicine didn't have a pill or a shot that would cure my seizures."

"I've heard that it's a slow process."

"You're not kidding. Since the accident, I've definitely learned patience. It was MJ's idea to get a service dog. The last thing I wanted to do was broadcast my disability, but MJ wouldn't give up on the idea. He saw a service dog in action at school, and he knew what they were capable of doing. He said he wouldn't worry about me so much if he knew I had a dog by my side."

"He was right, you know."

"I know. He led me to Jed, and Jed led me to you. I'm thankful every day for the two of you coming into my life."

I was touched by his words. I felt like Mark was telling me things he never shared with anyone else. After our sandwiches, we put the dogs back on leash and walked some of the paths. We stopped to talk with a family whose three small children wanted to pet the dogs. As we started back down the path, I said, "That little one was so cute. I had to fight the urge not to hug her."

"How long did you and your husband try to get pregnant?"

"We struggled for seven years."

"Seven years. That's a long time."

"It takes time to get appointments with specialists and try procedures. The maddening part is that none of the doctors could give me a definitive reason why I wasn't getting pregnant. We were nearing the end of our medical options when Jack got sick, and then that became our new reality."

He gave me a hug and said, "I'm sorry you had to go through that."

"I appreciate hearing that. No one ever knows what to say. Our family and friends didn't understand the roller coaster of emotions we went through every month. Jack and I were our only support. Every month we lived through the hope and anticipation of a new cycle, along with the pain and frustration when that cycle ended. The loss was so deep that it changed me. I stopped looking at babies, and I tried hard not to be around pregnant women and mothers. Even now, the worst day of the year for me is Mother's Day."

"Did you think about adopting?" Mark asked.

"We did, and we might have, but then we found out about Jack's cancer."

"You would have been a fantastic mother."

"Thank you for saying that. I don't think anyone's ever said that to me before. Jack would have been an amazing father if he had had the chance."

"Life isn't fair."

"I battled with fairness for a long time. I decided to quit questioning it and just go with it. Our lives are full of detours, and all we can do is keep moving and maneuver around them the best we can."

"You are an inspiration."

"So are you."

My first student, bringing her test paper up to my desk, interrupts me. I look out over my class and wonder what life has in store for them. Am I looking at the next president, rock star, or cancer victim? Like them, I don't know what the future holds, but I do know what I want right now. Whenever the opportunity comes, I want to be with Mark. I think we are both willing to see where this leads. I have a feeling this could be a very special Thanksgiving.

CHAPTER 23

MARK LANCER

The weather today has been crisp and raw. It feels like snow, even though none is in the forecast. Jed and I are sitting on the porch, waiting for Haley. We do this every time she comes. It's the least I can do.

Haley offered to do the cooking, thank goodness. I wouldn't know where to start with this meal. She instructed me about what groceries I should buy, but I have a feeling she's going to be bringing some things with her. Although I have very little cooking expertise, I plan on helping her in the kitchen.

I have been looking forward to Thanksgiving since Haley said she would come. Notoriously, I hate holidays unless I get to spend them with MJ. But spending Thanksgiving with Haley has changed that. I haven't felt this energized and alive in a long time.

I'm beginning to worry a bit as I keep checking the time. Haley is going to arrive later than I anticipated. Jed, sensing my mood, keeps nudging me to be petted. It didn't take him long to learn how to calm me down. Finally, I see her car turning the corner and coming down the street. I hurry off the porch to open her car door for her. As she gets out, she sighs with relief. I greet her with a kiss and wrap her in my arms. I feel her sigh again as she leans into me.

"Traffic?" I ask.

Stepping back, she looks up at me. "Thanksgiving Day, it's to be expected. Plus, I had to stop twice for Magic. She just wouldn't settle down. I think she knew she was coming to see Jed."

"Let me bring your bags in while you take the dogs out back."

"Thanks. The dogs will appreciate that."

I take the bag of food and dog stuff to the kitchen and return for her duffel bag. Not knowing what she is thinking, I'm not sure where to put it. I decide to leave it by the table in the hallway next to the stairs. I don't want her to feel any pressure from me. She knows where I stand. The next play is hers.

I find her in the middle of the yard, all three dogs vying for her attention. I stop on the deck and watch her with them. She is talking to them and laughing at their antics. I can't imagine a more beautiful sight.

She looks over and sees me watching her and joins me on the deck. "There is nothing more carefree and joyous than dogs at play. We can learn a lot from them," she says thoughtfully.

I put my arms around her, and she leans back into me as we watch the dogs.

"Well, are you ready to make your first turkey?" she asks.

"Lead the way. I'm at your command," I answer.

"Oh, I think I'm going to like this," she says playfully.

For the rest of the afternoon, she leads me through the preparations for our dinner. With the dogs underfoot and Haley very much in control, I never knew cooking could be so much fun. The football games I'm missing are totally forgotten with the kisses and playful teasing I'm receiving from Haley.

Later we are able to squeeze in a late-afternoon dog walk and a quick glance at the football scores while the turkey is cooking. At six-thirty, with the dogs fed and settled, we sit down in the dining room to eat. Having helped Haley in the kitchen, I have a greater appreciation for the time and effort that has gone into this meal.

Before we start eating, Haley takes my hands and says, "It's Thanksgiving, and I want to give thanks. Is that OK?"

This doesn't surprise me about her. Haley seems like the type of person who would have deep faith. Although I haven't practiced a religion for many years, I have always felt it was a part of my life. "Absolutely," I answer.

Smiling at me across the table, she says, "I am thankful for my life and all the blessings in it. I'm thankful that I was asked to be Jed's puppy raiser. Although I went into it kicking and screaming, it was one of the best decisions I ever made. Raising Jed was a challenge and an adventure that I will never forget. Seeing him work with you brings me tremendous joy and satisfaction. I am grateful that my dogs and I are here sharing this Thanksgiving dinner with you and Jed. I feel blessed that you came into my life and into my heart."

Moved by her words, I take a deep breath and give her hands a squeeze. "You're a hard act to follow."

"It's OK. You don't have to," she says.

"No, I want to. Just give me a minute."

I try to arrange my thoughts, hoping they will come out the way I want them to. "I am thankful for my son. He has made me so proud and so humble. I hope you get to meet him someday. I'm thankful that this new medication seems to be working and that it's been two weeks since my last seizure. I'm thankful for Jed. He has given me my life back, and he's led me to you. You captivated me the first time I met you, and I can't imagine my life without you in it."

She leans over the table and kisses me. "Happy Thanksgiving," she says.

"To the best one ever," I add.

Since I'm used to eating alone, I usually eat fast to get it over with. Most of the time, I watch the news or sports during dinner. Today, I remind myself to slow down and savor the food and company. Thanksgiving dinner has always been one of my favorite meals. But more importantly, I want to enjoy every minute of Haley's visit.

"Everything is really good, and I didn't manage to get in your way and mess anything up," I say.

"You were a great help in the kitchen. It is so much more fun than cooking alone," Haley responds.

With the dogs lounging under the table, ever hopeful, we talk about our everyday lives. Haley always seems to have some interesting school stories to share, and I usually can match her with some of my work tales. We linger at the table, talking and discussing our plans for the next few days.

"Would you like to go to the movies? There are a couple of good ones out now," I ask.

"I think I would rather just stay in and maybe catch something on TV. My dogs are great in new places, but I'm not comfortable leaving them here by themselves yet," Haley responds.

"Staying in works for me. I do have a couple of new places where we can walk the dogs and a few sights around town I haven't shown you yet. Also, I would like to take you out for dinner."

"We'll have plenty of leftovers for tomorrow night. Let's go out Saturday," Haley suggests. "By then, my dogs will be more familiar with your house. They're usually not destructive, but you never know."

After deciding that dessert can wait until later, we clean up the dishes and take the dogs for a walk. It is cold and dark as we make our way around the neighborhood. The dogs love exploring all the new smells and are not bothered by the cold. We are both quiet during the walk. I wonder what Haley is thinking, and I wonder how the night will play out.

"You're quiet this evening," I say.

"It's a beautiful night and the best Thanksgiving I've had in a long time. Since Jack died, holidays have always been days that I just needed to get through," she says. "Thank you for making this one special again."

"I had a lot of trouble with holidays too. But then, you make every day special for me."

Looking over at me with a smile, she says, "You're a kind man."

"No. Just a truthful one," I respond. As we continue our walk, I look down at Jed on my left and then over at Haley on my right. I feel like my life is in balance again, and I know I'm a lucky man.

When we get back to the house, I light a fire in the living room fireplace, and that's where we enjoy our dessert. I have a large sheepskin rug on the floor, and when we're done eating, we join the dogs there. I like a fire. There is something about it that is contemplative and primitive. As we watch the flames and listen to them crackle and hiss, I can't help asking her, "What are you thinking?"

She looks back at me and says, "Tell me something about yourself that I don't know."

"That takes some thought," I answer, giving myself time to think. "OK, here goes. When I was growing up, my dream was to be a major-league baseball player. When I was little, I slept with a baseball cradled in my hand and my bat and glove beside my bed. That way, if there was an emergency during the night, I could escape with my most valuable possessions. Everywhere I went, my bat, ball, and glove accompanied me. Every chance I got, I wanted to practice or play. My poor dad, he barely made it home from work, and I was begging him to pitch batting practice or hit ground balls to me. I don't know how he did it, but he always made time for me. He never missed one of my games in Little League, high school, or college. My mother, either. I ended up being good enough to play in college but not good enough to be drafted. I did go to some Major League open tryouts, but nothing came of it. Before the accident, I played for our police league. Now, I'm just an avid fan who never lost his love for the game." After a pause, I say, "OK. It's your turn. Same question."

"Well . . ." She pauses with a sheepish grin. "I've found out the hard way that I'm claustrophobic. I don't like to be closed in. One day when I was training Jed, we got stuck in an elevator in one of the stores at the mall. It didn't even start to move yet. We were just stuck on the ground floor. I was in a state of panic, hitting the help button and screaming. The only way I got myself under control was by thinking that if I kept this behavior up, I might permanently scar Jed. He, on the other hand, looked at the episode as a whole new adventure. Within ten minutes, we were rescued. It didn't affect Jed in any way, but I've been a mess ever since. Now I try never to use elevators. If I have to use one, and there are more than three people in it, I won't get in. If more people enter than I'm comfortable with, I've been known to plow them down to get off. Unfortunately, it carried over to flying. Compounding my other bad experiences in planes, now, I find that the longer I'm in a plane, the more it starts closing in on me. You really don't want to fly with me. I'm in a state of panic the whole time."

"So, I guess a vacation to Australia wouldn't go over well?"

Haley laughs and says, "You would probably have to knock me out for that."

We are quiet for a while, thinking about what we just shared. Then I say, "OK, my turn. Answer this one for me. What is the best advice you ever received?"

"Oh, I got this one. No regrets. My grandmother always told me to live my life so I end up with no regrets. I think about that every time I make a decision, especially a big one. So far, it has guided me well." She pauses and then inquires, "What about you?"

"'Keep your promises,' my dad used to say to me. 'A man is only as good as his word.' My dad lived by this philosophy every day of his life. I can't remember a time when he didn't follow through on a promise. I was glad he wasn't around to see my divorce. I took my vows seriously and planned on honoring them despite the difficulties we were having. I made a commitment to Melissa, and I would have honored it to the day I died. Unfortunately, she didn't feel the same way."

After a brief pause, Haley says, "OK, here's another one. What is your biggest fear?"

"That's an easy one. That my doctors won't find the proper medication for me and I will have seizures for the rest of my life. Getting Jed and meeting you has lessened the prominence of fear that I used to experience. I really miss driving, though. Cars have always been a big part of my life." I get up and add some wood to the fire before I ask: "And you? What's your biggest fear?"

"That I haven't done enough with what I've been given. That I haven't cared enough, that I haven't helped people enough, that I haven't been kind enough, that somehow my bad will outweigh my good."

Shaking my head in disbelief, I look at her, "I can't imagine you doing anything bad. I'm a cop, and I've seen bad. You're a teacher. Your life is devoted to others."

"You're in law enforcement. So is yours."

"I admit it. I like to see the good guys win."

"You get to make that happen."

"Sometimes, but not as much as I would like," I add.

We are quiet for a time. The fire seems to have stolen our words, and we are both lost in thought. Finally, I put into words what I've wanted to know all day. "My turn for a question."

"OK. Go ahead."

Looking at her lovely face bathed by the firelight, I ask, "What bedroom are you planning to use tonight?"

Haley doesn't respond. Looking me straight in the eyes, she stands, takes my hand, and heads for the stairs. At the top of the stairs, she turns toward my bedroom. When I see where she is heading, I lift her off her feet and carry her the rest of the way.

"I like that answer," I manage to say in between kisses.

"I thought you would," Haley responds with a smile.

"Should I use a condom?" I ask.

"If I get pregnant, it would be a miracle," she responds.

"Miracles happen," I say. "I found you."

We are both done talking. We let our actions take over for our words. Now is the time for touching, feeling, and giving. As I gently lay her on the bed, she begins to unbutton my shirt. I am overwhelmed with emotion. I feel like everything I've gone through in the last four years has been leading up to this moment with this woman. I am humbled by Haley's gift of love. I don't know what I've done to deserve it. I never want to stop holding her, pleasing her, or loving her. She has come into my life, and I will never be the same.

CHAPTER 24

HALEY DUNCAN

It is the middle of the night, and I wake to the feel of Mark beside me. Surprisingly, all the dogs are on the floor somewhere, so the bed is just ours. I look over at Mark and watch him sleep. I remain still, savoring this moment in time and letting my feelings flow.

It is always special the first time you love someone. Tonight with Mark feels like a promise that whispers of hope for times to come. I feel closer to him now, a deep closeness that will become a part of me. Where I thought I might be vulnerable, I feel a security that wasn't there before. We've now created a bond that only belongs to the two of us.

I have been loved by two men in my life. If I were to shut my eyes, I could call up their touch and experience it all over again. I could tell them apart instantly. Each man has his own way of loving.

Jack was the love of my youth. We taught each other how to give love and receive it. We grew together, learned from each other, and became secure in our bond. It saw us through my infertility and Jack's cancer. It never crossed my mind that we wouldn't grow old together. It is still hard for me to believe that the end of our marriage was so sad and tragic. But it didn't stop the love. My love for Jack didn't end with his death. It is just buried in my heart now and will always be a part of me.

I see Mark through a grown woman's eyes. I love him with a passion and maturity that only life's tragedies could awaken in me. Knowing now how fragile and uncertain life can be, I love him like this is the first and last time. I hope his love is my future. In Mark, I've found another wounded heart. Together, I believe, we can heal each other and make each other whole again.

I have always felt that the promise of love comes from the touch, not the words. Words seem so unnecessary when you're making or showing love. An arm around your shoulder, a hand in a hand, a touch of one's hair, body against body—these gestures always tell me more than words ever could. This is strange for me, considering words are my livelihood. But touch is a language all its own, and I savor everything that it is telling me.

It's telling me that I can love again. I feel it, and I relish in the giddiness of it. Without either of us saying "I love you," I feel our hearts have made a commitment to each other and that our lives are now intertwined. I feel Mark's love for me. I see it in his eyes when he looks at me, and I feel it in his touch. I believe we can have our "happily ever after." I'm planning on it now. I hope he is too.

CHAPTER 25

MARK LANCER

S ilently I get out of bed, reluctant to leave Haley for even a minute. Jed needs to go out, and I'm trying to get Magic and Thunder to join us and let her sleep. The first light of morning is breaking as I stand on the deck, watching the dogs. It is cold, and I can see my breath and feel the wind through the light jacket I threw on. I'm hoping the dogs are quick with their business. I can't wait to get back to Haley.

As I watch the light take over the night sky, it makes me think of how Haley has removed the darkness from my life. Her brightness and warmth radiate from her and seep into me. For the rest of my life, I could be happy just to bask in her glow. She sparked a flame in me that only she can control. This is a totally new feeling for me. Haley shows me a life of possibilities and second chances. She makes me feel whole again. I don't think I have ever felt this way about a woman before. I've never taken love casually like so many men do. Haley is only the second woman I've slept with. She and my ex-wife could not be more different in who they are and in how they love. Last night, I felt like I couldn't give enough of myself to Haley. I can find myself getting lost in her.

I feel arms around me, and I notice that Haley slipped my shirt on to come outside. "Come here. You must be cold," I say as I move her in front of me and wrap my arms around her. "My shirt looks a lot better on you."

"I think I have to disagree with you," she says.

"I didn't want to wake you. As soon as I left, I missed you," I tell her.

"Even though I didn't hear you, I felt you leave me. The bed is too big without you," she replies.

"I was trying to hurry them. Couldn't you teach your own dogs to go on command like Jed?" I ask.

Shaking her head slightly, she responds, "Jed is spoiling you."

"So are you. I'm a lucky man. A great dog by my side and a beautiful woman in my bed."

"I feel lucky too. Come back to bed. I'm not ready to get up yet," Haley says.

"I don't think I ever will be," I answer.

CHAPTER 26

HALEY DUNCAN

I breathe a sigh of relief as I pull into my parents' Florida home. I grab my phone and send Mark a quick text. He always feels better when he knows I've arrived safely. Mom and Cassie open the front door, and I enter, rolling my carry-on and another piece of luggage behind me.

We exchange kisses and hugs. "Where are Dad, Mike, and the kids?" I ask, looking around for them.

"Beach walk. You know the kids. They're not much for sitting around," Cassie answers. "How was your flight?"

"It was smooth, thank goodness. Two hours is doable. After that, I start to get shaky, especially when I'm traveling alone."

Mom shakes her head. "I hate that you are flying alone."

"Well, since I had to leave the dogs at home, alone it is," I answer as we head for the kitchen. "The tree looks real, even if it's not. Everything is decorated beautifully, Mom," I remark. "It's still hard celebrating Christmas when the weather is in the seventies down here."

"It doesn't take long to get used to this weather, dear," Mom responds. "I put some snacks out in case you're hungry."

Fruit, cheese, and crackers are on the kitchen island, and the three of us gather around there, nibbling on the goodies.

"So, you look good," Cassie says to me. "How is everything going?"

"Things are great. I'm happy," I say with a smile.

"Is this due to a certain someone?" Cassie asks.

"Someone? Who is someone?" Mom immediately chimes in, looking somewhat confused.

"Didn't Haley tell you, Mom?" Cassie looks at me with a question in her eyes.

I shoot her a look and then turn to my mother and say, "I'm seeing someone."

"Seeing someone, like dating someone?" Mom asks, a little startled. "Why am I just now hearing about this?"

"Mom, I didn't want you to worry and bombard me with a hundred questions," I say, looking over at Cassie with a grimace that says we'll talk about this later.

"Haley, you know I only want what's best for both my girls. You're young and beautiful. Of course, you'll marry again."

"Mom, we're just dating," I say.

"Cassie, did you know about this?" Mom asks, looking at her as if she's to blame.

"Way to go, Haley. Now you're getting me in trouble," Cassie says, letting me know that this is my fault, not hers.

"Well, tell me about him. Who is he? What does he do for a living? How did you meet him?" Mom asks all in one breath.

"His name is Mark Lancer, and he's a state policeman."

Before Haley can get the next words out, Mom breaks in, "Oh, Haley, you didn't get stopped for a speeding ticket, did you?"

"No, Mom. He's the man who was matched with Jed, the service dog I raised," I reply.

"But you told me that Jed went to a man who has seizures," Mom says with confusion.

"He did. He went to Mark, and that's whom I'm dating. Jed, by the way, is doing remarkable work. He's becoming pretty good at alerting Mark to his seizures. Mark's medications seem to be working better too. He hasn't had a seizure this month yet," I state.

"He still can't drive yet, can he?" Cassie asks.

"He has to go a year without a seizure for the doctors to permit him to get his license back," I respond.

"I thought you told me that Jed was moving across the state to live," Mom says. I can see she is still trying to process all this new information.

"That's right," I respond, trying to keep things vague.

"Well?" Mom says, waiting for an explanation.

"Mark and Jed live four hours away," Cassie interjects, and I can't help shooting her that "you're not helping matters" look.

"Oh, Haley, tell me you don't drive all that way alone just for a man?" Mom asks with worry in her voice.

"I'm never alone. I have Magic and Thunder with me."

"So, how is Mark spending Christmas?" Cassie asks.

"He flew to California to see his son, who is enrolled in med school there. Because of Jed, he felt comfortable enough to make the trip," I answer with a bit of an edge in my voice.

"So he has a son," Mom remarks. "Are there other children? What happened to his wife? There was a wife, I hope?"

"Just the one son, and he's been divorced for five years," I reply.

"Are you sure this is the type of man you want to get involved with?" Mom asks with a worried look on her face.

"Mom, I'm thirty-nine years old. I'm not a teenager going on my first date."

"Now, Haley, don't get like that," Mom responds.

"Listen, I have been numb since Jack died. Raising Jed and meeting Mark are the best things that have happened to me since. I feel alive again. I feel loved again. I can't see the future. I don't know if Mark and I will end up together. But I know one thing. I want to see this through."

"Haley dear, I just don't want to see you hurt again," Mom says, grabbing my hand.

I look at her hand over mine and then into her eyes. "If he breaks my heart, so be it. I'll live through it. I've had some practice with this already. Who knows, I might end up breaking his."

"You know I only have your best interests at heart," Mom says as she rounds the island and gives me a hug.

"I know that," I reply, hugging her back.

Right then, the kitchen door bursts open, and the rest of the family returns from their beach walk. The kitchen is filled with their chatter.

"Aunt Haley's here."

"Aunt Haley, look at my shell."

"Grandma, Grandpa is tired."

"Mom, I'm hungry."

I look over at Cassie with relief in my eyes. I finger the necklace that Mark gave me for Christmas. I remember his words as he put it around my neck. "Your bracelet needed a friend. Everything in life is better in pairs."

Mom and Dad, Cassie and Mike with their four children, and me. I feel the imbalance. Looking around at everyone gathered in the kitchen, I hear my mother say, "We're all here. Let Christmas begin."

Wishing Mark was here with me, I put a smile on my face and join the festivities.

CHAPTER 27

MARK LANCER

Flying out to California to spend the Christmas holiday with MJ is something I thought I might never do again. Jed made this happen. I guess I need to give the medications some credit too, but if it wasn't for Jed, I know I wouldn't be attempting this trip. It took a while for me to trust his instincts, but he hasn't let me down yet.

When I booked my flight, I alerted the airline that I would be traveling with my service dog. They gave me some instructions and verified that Jed gets a free ride. On the day of the flight, they strongly suggested that we arrive early at the airport. Well, that was a no-brainer. Because this will be our first trip together, I am taking every precaution I can to make sure things go as smoothly as possible.

The airport is busy when we arrive, and that adds to my nervousness. I know Jed is picking up on this. He has become extremely sensitive to my moods and emotions. I find him giving me more eye contact than usual and walking closer to my leg. The sights and sounds of the airport don't seem to faze him, and I wonder if a trip to the airport was part of his training.

Jed certainly attracts attention everywhere we go. People are usually curious but respectful. As we walk past a family with young children, I hear the mother say, "He's a working dog. You can't pet him."

Smiling at them, we continue on our way. Most of the time, this is true, but there are times when I do give permission for Jed to be greeted and petted. Not today, though. This is a new adventure for both of us.

When we arrive at the check-in counter, we meet Susan, an airline representative.

"This is Jed, my service dog. Here is the required documentation," I say as I pull it out of my pocket.

"Thank you. This will only take a moment. I am required to follow the airline's procedures and guidelines," she says as she checks my papers.

The documentation identifies Jed as my service dog and not an emotional support animal. Most people don't understand the difference. A service dog is trained to perform jobs related to its owner's disability. An emotional support dog, or ESD, as they are often referred to, merely provides comfort to its owner in some way. Jed, by law, is permitted everywhere I go. An emotional support dog does not always have this privilege. My medical papers explain to Susan my seizures and the job Jed does for me.

"Everything is in order. I hope you have a pleasant flight and a wonderful holiday," she says as she sends us on our way.

Our next stop is airport security. Just like everyone else, Jed is screened along with me. Not only do I remove my shoes and belt, but Jed's collar and leash have to come off as well. I notice a lot of people smiling and pointing at us as we walk through the scanner together. I realize it is Jed who is the celebrity here and not me.

At the boarding gate, I introduce myself to Mary, the airline attendant. "You have a beautiful Lab there," she says. "I have one at home, but he's a yellow. They're great dogs."

"The best," I answer.

She checks our tickets and lets us board the airplane first. This surprises me, and I stroke Jed's head in thanks. I can get used to this first-class treatment.

When I booked my ticket, I made sure I got a seat in the first row. The airline assured me that this row provides the most legroom, which means more space for Jed. As I settle in my seat, Jed finds his spot halfway under the seat and halfway between my legs. He seems comfortable, and it won't surprise me if he naps most of the way there. I sit back and let out a sigh of relief.

This has gone better than I expected. Check another first off my bucket list.

As I put my head back and relax, I have time to let my thoughts drift to Haley, and I wonder how her plane flight is going. I am glad we are both spending the holiday with our respective families, but I'll miss her all the same. We celebrated our own first Christmas together last weekend. It was a special time for us, but then again, Haley makes everything special.

It gives me great pleasure to see her wearing the bracelet I gave her. So for her Christmas present, I designed a necklace to match. I'm pretty sure she liked it. Since I placed it around her neck, I haven't seen it off her yet. All weekend, I noticed that she touched it often, moving the stone between her fingers, a happy smile on her face. It's nice knowing that I put it there.

I reach down in my backpack and lift out the new tablet Haley gave me for Christmas. I remember how surprised she was that I didn't have one.

"I couldn't survive without my tablet. Wait till you start using it. You will wonder how you managed to live without one for so long," she said.

Haley set it up for me and even downloaded some games she thought I would enjoy on my trip. She then went into teacher mode and gave me a basic lesson on usage. I have a feeling I am going to like this new gadget, especially because it came from her.

Both of us included the dogs in our Christmas celebration. There were plenty of bones and new toys for all three. I don't know what kind of research goes into these dog toys, but the talking ball was the hit of the evening. Haley and I laughed at all three dogs trying to figure out what to do with it.

After opening our presents, we sat together in front of the fire with the dogs at our feet. As Christmas songs played, we enjoyed the lights coming from the small tree we decorated earlier.

"I love the music of Christmas," I can hear Haley saying. "I could listen to it all year long."

The flight starts to get a little bumpy, but it doesn't seem to bother Jed. I wonder if it is any different for him than riding on the bus or in a car. Trying to master some of these games Haley downloaded makes the trip seem shorter than it really is. Before I know it, we are touching down in California.

Once the plane stops and they take care of all the safety procedures, Jed and I are permitted to disembark first. Again, I ruffle his ears in thanks, enjoying the perks he brings.

As Jed and I maneuver through the walkway and enter the terminal, I see MJ standing at the rope, waiting for us. As I look at my son, I'm overwhelmed with emotion. It's been five months since he visited me last summer, and it's so good to see him again. We embrace in greeting, and as we move apart, I say, "Let me introduce you to Jed."

MJ goes down to Jed's level, smiling at him.

"It's OK. You can pet him. He's heard a lot about you so far. He'll probably recognize your voice from our FaceTime."

"Jed, it's finally a pleasure to meet you," MJ says as he pets him under his neck. "Wait until you see what I have planned for us over the next five days. I hope you two are up for it."

I think about spending the next five days with my son. For some reason, that Styx song plays in my mind, "These Are the Best of Times."

CHAPTER 28

HALEY DUNCAN

The end of winter is finally approaching. March always carries the promise of brighter skies and warmer days. It's been a rough winter in more ways than one. My visits to Mark have been curtailed by ice and snow and my school activities. We were both disappointed that I could only make it out there twice in January and once in February. Since Mark's six-month evaluation was in February, he and Jed rode back with me from that visit. Even though they only stayed for two nights, it was a nice change having them here. Unfortunately, they had to take the bus back home. It made for a long, tiring day for them.

We both are learning the difficulties of a long-distance relationship. If we had years behind us as a couple, things would be a lot easier. Being apart more than being together makes it difficult to learn about each other. Although we're in contact every day, it just doesn't seem to be enough. I worry about this as I pack for the weekend.

It has been two weeks since Mark and I have been together. The ride out there seems longer than normal. I arrive around 7:30 p.m. and look for Mark and Jed. Despite the weather, they are always sitting on the front porch, waiting for us. Mark greets me with a big hug and kiss. As I am folded in his arms, all my worries are gone, allowing me to focus on the now.

Since it is late when we arrive, Mark usually has some kind of sandwiches ready for us. I don't know how he does it, but he always has some little surprise waiting for me also. He must be using his investigative skills because he manages to come up with something special every time I visit. One week it was daisies, my favorite flower. Another week it was the novel I wanted to read. This week it is a framed picture of the five of us at the park.

"Can I bother you to take our picture?" Mark had asked a young couple strolling by us one Saturday.

"Absolutely," the young man answered as Mark handed him his phone. "You asked the right person. I'm into photography."

He went out of his way to pose us, using the woods as a backdrop. It's not easy to get the attention of three dogs, but somehow he managed it. The picture is a keepsake.

Saturday morning dawns bright and sunny and full of plans. Mark decides to make pancakes for us, so I busy myself scrambling some eggs. In the middle of our cooking, his cell phone rings. After looking at the caller ID, he excuses himself from the kitchen.

"I'm sorry about that," he says as he returns. "That was Sergeant Dean. We have an emergency situation, and he's asking me to report. Don't worry. It's not a disaster or anything like that. It has to do with this investigation I'm involved in."

"No problem," I quickly respond. "I'll take you. Do you have time to eat?"

"If you finish up the cooking while I get dressed, I can probably eat something quick," Mark replies.

On the way to the station, Mark is silent. I can't help myself from asking, "You're quiet. Are you worried about your investigation?"

"No. I'm worried about you. You drove all this way, and we both made plans for the day, and now the whole weekend might be gone."

"I understand work responsibilities," I say. "Especially with the kind of work you do. I'll be OK, really. Let me know if you need a ride back."

When I pull into the station and park, Mark leans over, takes my face between his hands, and kisses me with such passion that it leaves me breathless. "Well, that should hold me all day," I manage to say.

"That's just a preview. We'll pick up from here later," he promises.

"I'll look forward to it," I say with a smile.

As soon as I arrive back at his house, I get the leashes and take Magic and Thunder for a walk. It is different walking around his neighborhood without him. I follow our usual route, and when I am almost back to his house, I hear, "Wow, you have two dogs." I stop and turn toward a small boy walking up to me.

"I do. They're buddies."

"Can I pet them?"

"Sure, this is Magic, and this one is Thunder."

"I wish I had a dog. My friend, Officer Mark, he has a black dog named Jed. He's a working dog. Officer Mark lets me pet Jed sometimes."

"I know Jed. I raised him from a puppy for Officer Mark."

Hearing the front door slam, I look up and see a well-dressed, well-endowed woman approaching us. Not knowing if she likes dogs, I pull Magic and Thunder closer to me.

"Hi. I don't think I know you. Are you from around here?" she inquires.

"No, I'm from the other side of the state," I respond.

"Are you visiting someone?"

"Yes," I reply, wondering why she is so interested.

"Mom, she says she knows Officer Mark, and she raised Jed as a puppy," the boy says.

"Oh, so you're visiting Mark?" she asks.

"I am."

"He is such a great guy and handsome too. It is so nice having him just down the street. He's handy if I have any house questions, and he has been so good with Brandon. Right, honey?" she says to the little boy.

"I really like Officer Mark," Brandon says.

"That doesn't surprise me," I respond as I start to move away with Magic and Thunder.

"Are you related to Mark?" she asks.

"No," I reply.

"Are you and Mark a couple?" she inquires.

"I guess you could call us that," I say.

"How long have you been together?"

"Awhile. Sorry, but I really must go. Bye, Brandon."

Walking the rest of the way to Mark's house, I feel her watching me. As I close the front door, I breathe a sigh of relief. This neighbor is just a bit too nosy for me. I find myself thinking about her living this close to Mark, and I find myself wishing she wasn't so attractive.

Since I have no idea how long Mark will be gone, I'm glad I brought schoolwork to do. I set up on the kitchen table and start grading essays. I pretty much spend the day there with breaks for lunch and playing with the dogs. I keep them out back. After meeting Brandon and his mother, I think I'll wait for any walks until Mark is with us.

He texts around five, "On the way home. Greg is dropping me off. I made dinner reservations."

I'm delighted he is done working, and I'm not surprised by the reservation. Mark usually takes me out for dinner on Saturday nights. The meals range anywhere from down-home country cooking to elegant dining. We go somewhere different each time since we both enjoy trying new restaurants. We haven't repeated any yet, so I wonder where it will be tonight. There seems to be a wealth of restaurants in the surrounding area for us to try.

When Mark and Jed walk in the front door, I can see how worn out Mark is from the day.

Before I can greet him with a hug, Jed turns and stands right in front of him, staring and alert. Mark immediately lowers himself down to the floor as I rush over. I cradle his head during the seizure. After a couple of minutes, the twitching stops, and Mark opens his eyes and orientates himself.

"Boy, I'm really blowing this weekend," he says.

"You're definitely going to have to make it up to me later," I tease.

"Just give me some time. I'll be fine for dinner," he replies.

"I'd rather have you fine for later," I say.

He laughs, sits up, and leans against the wall. Magic and Thunder have now joined us and relish the fact that we're all on the floor at the perfect level for them to give some wet kisses.

"Let's stay in tonight. We can grab something here or call out for pizza," I suggest.

"But I always take you out on Saturday night. I made reservations at this new place," he says.

"Cancel them. Call for a pizza instead. You've had a long day, and I'm tired from all the essays I've been grading. Let's just relax here and enjoy being together."

"If that's what you want," Mark says as I see the relief in his eyes.

"That's what I want," I reply. "But I do have something in mind for dessert," I say as I lean over and kiss him.

"Care to tell me what it is?" Mark says, grinning as he kisses me back.

"Later," I reply. "Now call for pizza, and let's get these dogs fed."

When the pizza arrives, we take it to the family room and settle in.

"Can you tell me anything about what you did today?" I ask.

"Not much," he replies. "I can tell you it has to do with an investigation I've been working on for over six months now. It's proving to be bigger and more involved than we ever imagined going in. We are coordinating with law enforcement from other states. I had no choice. I had to be there today."

"Well, whatever it is, I hope you get the bad guys and it has a happy ending."

"Happy ending? That's an interesting way to put it."

"I believe in happy endings."

"I wish I did."

Later, as we lie in each other's arms, I think about happy endings.

"I met two of your admirers today," I say.

"I have two admirers?" He looks at me dumbfounded.

"Brandon and his mother."

"Oh no. Did she bombard you with questions?"

"Pretty much."

"I'm sorry. I should have warned you about her."

"Brandon is adorable. I wouldn't mind taking him home with me."

"He's a great kid. You can't help but like him."

"I can see where men wouldn't mind liking his mother either."

"I guess."

"Does she have a name?"

"Alexandra Jennings."

"Well, Alexandra Jennings is a beautiful woman."

"I guess. If you like her type."

"What type is that?" I inquire.

"Not my type," Mark answers.

"What is your type?" I ask.

"You," he answers with a kiss on the top of my head.

"She asked if we were a couple," I say before he distracts me with more of his kisses.

"What did you say?"

"I said I guess you can call us that."

"You guess?" he inquires.

"We've never talked about it," I answer.

"I didn't think it needed to be said," Mark replies.

"I'm an English teacher. I live by words."

Mark sits up and leans over me. Looking directly into my eyes, he says, "Then listen to these words. I love you, Haley Duncan, and I definitely consider us a couple."

Tracing my fingers down the side of his face, I answer, "I love you, Mark Lancer, and we're going to have a happy ending." There are no more words to be said tonight.

Sunday morning dawns a cool, overcast day. Trying not to wake Mark, I slide out of bed and head for the bathroom. On Sundays, I like to go to church. My parents were very devoted Christians, and they took Cassie and me to church every week. On one of our neighborhood dog walks, I discovered a small church close to Mark's house. It became a habit for me to get up and walk to the early service every Sunday. Since Mark is not practicing a religion, he always had breakfast ready and waiting for me when I got back.

When I return to the bedroom, I find Mark out of bed and dressing in nice clothes. I ask him, "Do you have to go back into work today?"

"No, I thought I would go to church with you," he replies.

"I would like that," I respond, surprised.

"I have had trouble returning to church since the accident," Mark says. "I couldn't find much in my life to be thankful for."

"And now?" I ask.

"Now, I have a lot to be thankful for," he says. "I find I want to go to church with you. You make things easier."

"I'm glad you're coming with me. We have a lot of reasons to be thankful," I reply.

Even though it looks like it might rain, we decided to walk the couple of blocks to the church. It is only half-filled, so we are able to get a spot up front and off to the side with plenty of room for Jed. After the service, we stop and greet the priest on the way out.

"I was gauging my sermon on your dog," the priest tells us. "When his eyes were open, I knew it was going well. When he started to snooze, I figured the congregation probably was too, so I'd better wrap it up." Mark and I both laugh over his comments. We assure the priest that we will be back.

When we return to the house, we sit down to cereal and the Sunday paper. Mark and I often get into a lively discussion about current events or other articles. It is interesting to hear Mark's perspective from the law enforcement angle. This is all new to me, and I find his work fascinating.

"So, where do you keep your gun?" I ask.

"Since the accident, it has been locked up at the station," he replies. "I'm not permitted to carry it until my seizures are under control. Growing up, I remember my dad always bringing his home with him. The first thing he did when he walked through the door was to lock it up. As far back as I can remember, he was teaching me about gun safety. I did the same with MJ, much to Melissa's dismay. She was never happy about a gun in the house. It didn't matter that I kept it in a safe stored in a locked closet."

Later that morning, we take the dogs for a walk around the neighborhood. I was secretly glad that we didn't run into Alexandra and Brandon again. Along the way, we did see some familiar people and their dogs.

"Here comes Rummy," Mark says. A golden doodle and its owner walks toward us.

"Looks like she got a haircut," I add.

We are ashamed to admit that we tend to remember the dogs' names before their owners. When we return from our walk, lunch is a bit subdued because leaving is on both of our minds. Regrettably, the dogs and I start for home after lunch. With the end of my school year quickly approaching, Mark and I have been making plans for the summer. He's given me the normal amount of teacher ribbing.

"It must be nice having the whole summer off," he says with a grin on his face.

"Really, are you sure you want to go there?" I ask.

"Law enforcement, on the other hand, works twenty-four hours a day every day of the year," he states, grinning all the more.

"Oh, please, are you done, or should I threaten to teach summer school?" I respond.

He grabs me and pulls me into his arms, laughing. "You wouldn't."

When he's finished teasing me about it, he admits that he has a nice amount of vacation time saved, and he plans to use it. A summer of togetherness is something we are both looking forward to. We've ruled out any big trips for the time being because of his seizures and plan on staying close to home. He and Jed are required to make the trip back to Homeland for their year-end testing. This means we will be spending part of the summer at my home too. I can't wait.

This will be a nice change.

Over the last nine months, I have found myself falling in love again. Although there are times when it feels like first love, it's nice to have the maturity of age and the wisdom of experience to guide me now. I have learned that the heart has a vast capacity for love. Healing truly does come if you give it time. Jack will always be a part of who I am. I still think of him every day. I believe he would be happy that I found someone. I feel like my life has taken so many detours from what I had originally planned for myself. But time moves on, and I hope I have a lot of living and loving yet ahead of me.

CHAPTER 29

MARK LANCER

It's been a long time since I've had a good summer, and this is turning into a great one. If only MJ could be here, it would be perfect. I never knew a relationship could be this easy. It certainly wasn't with Melissa. Now that Haley and I are together, with no distance between us, it seems like the pieces of my life are all falling into place. I hate to leave for work in the morning, and I can't wait to get home at night. There is a rhythm to my days with her. She and her dogs fill the house with energy and life.

Instead of any big summer trips, we decide to be Pittsburgh tourists. Together, we make a list of all the attractions we want to visit. There's a lot to see and do in my city.

"Pirates game?" I ask.

"Absolutely. You love baseball. You can teach me how to score," she said.

"Point State Park? It has one of the country's largest fountains and is located on the tip of the Golden Triangle at the junction of the Allegheny and Monongahela Rivers and the birth of the Ohio."

"That sounds like a great place to take the dogs. Let's pack a picnic lunch and make a day of it. It must be beautiful there by the rivers, and with three water dogs, it could be interesting."

"How about the Strip District?" I ask.

"Excuse me?" Haley says.

"It's not what you think. It's a renovated part of the city that is now home to shopping, art, dining, and all kinds of markets. It is very touristy."

"Well, that sounds better. Add it to the list."

"You probably don't want to ride the Duquesne Incline?"

"Why not?" she asks.

"Didn't you tell me you were claustrophobic?"

"It depends. Show me a picture of it." To my surprise, after looking at the cable car, Haley said, "I can do that."

"OK. It just made the list."

As the summer moves on, we are whittling away at our list of major attractions. I am seeing my city in a new way with Haley and Jed by my side. Haley makes everything fun. We still have the Carnegie Museum of Art, the Carnegie Science Center, and the Phipps Conservatory on our list, and a lot of summer to go.

It is tradition for Greg, my ex-partner, to host a Fourth of July picnic at his home. It's usually the same gang every year—mostly fellow troopers from work and a few friends and neighbors. Even Sergeant Dean has been known to show up. This year, when I responded yes to the invitation, saying two would be attending, Greg took it as a joke. He thought I was including Jed as my guest. When he asked me about it at work the next day, I said I was bringing a lady friend.

"What? Who is this lady friend? Do I know her?" Greg asked.

"No, you don't know her," I replied.

"Well, who is she?"

"Her name is Haley Duncan."

"That's not telling me much."

"She was Jed's puppy raiser."

"Is this some type of training?"

"No."

"Well?"

"Well, what?"

"You mean you're seeing her, like a date?" he asked.

"I'm definitely seeing her. She's staying with me for the summer," I replied.

I know this took him by surprise. We talk regularly at work and eat lunch together when he's on the day shift, and I've never mentioned Haley.

Looking at me intently, he asked, "What's she like?"

"You'll like her. Everyone does. You'll meet her at the picnic," I responded.

The phone interrupted our conversation, and he didn't have the opportunity to bring it up again. I'm sure he's curious about this woman in my life, and I'm certain he's going to check Haley out at the picnic.

Luckily the day of the picnic is beautiful, with no rain in sight. The party is starting to get into full swing when Haley, Jed, and I arrive. I make a point to introduce Haley to my friends since everyone is curious about her. Along with Jed, we generate a lot of attention from the other guests.

I see Greg standing on the deck, so we make our way over to him. "Greg, this is Haley."

"Haley, it's nice to meet you," Greg says, offering her his hand.

"Haley, this is Greg, our host and my best friend," I say.

"Greg, thank you for inviting us," Haley says, shaking his hand. "Mark mentioned that he hasn't attended your picnic for a number of years," she adds, giving me a glance and a smile.

I return her smile and move closer to her, putting my hand on her back. She looks at Greg and says, "You have a beautiful home. How long have you lived here?"

She seems relaxed and comfortable in this setting, which surprises me. We troopers can be a pretty intimidating lot if you don't know us. "Ten years," Greg answers. "It's been a work in progress."

"Homes always are," she responds.

Sergeant Dean has made his way over to us, and as I start the introductions, I notice that Greg's wife is motioning to him from the house. He reluctantly excuses himself and misses the rest of our conversation.

As the party progresses, I feel Greg keeping an eye on us. Later, when Haley and Jed are standing under the elm tree while I play horseshoes, I'm not surprised to see Greg making his way over to her. Even though I act like I'm not paying attention, I eavesdrop on their conversation.

As Greg approaches, Haley says, "Hi, Greg. This is a wonderful picnic."

"I'm surprised you remembered my name. You must have met over thirty new people so far today," Greg responds.

"I'm a teacher. I have to specialize in learning names," she answers.

"Are you having a good time?" he asks.

"I am," she replies.

"You know I haven't seen Mark this relaxed in a long time. You must be good for him."

"I hope so, but Jed is really the one responsible. These service dogs continually amaze me with their ability to help people live full, independent lives."

"You might be right. I admit, I had my doubts when Mark told me he was paying five thousand dollars for a dog."

"Well, not everyone has to pay the full amount. There are scholarships and funds available to help disabled people who can't afford it. Many of our veterans receive their dogs free through donations from different organizations or through grant money. To tell you the truth, five thousand dollars is only a portion of the cost of a service dog. Twenty thousand dollars is more like the actual cost of raising, training, and placing each service dog."

"Twenty thousand dollars? Really?" Greg responds.

"Yes. The Homeland Service Dog Association, where Mark got Jed, breeds the Labrador retrievers they use. Their food, care, in-depth health screenings, neutering or spaying, and rigorous training program costs money. I think there are about twelve full-time people on staff. But the program couldn't survive without their volunteers, like me."

"Why Labs?" he asks.

"For the same reason that your police dogs are usually German shepherds or Belgian Malinois. Labs are suited perfectly for service work. They have few health problems, need limited grooming, have a patient, calm temperament, and generally love everyone."

"How did you get involved with all of this?" he inquires.

"I love dogs, and I wanted to be active with them during my summer vacations. I heard about the work of this organization, and I wanted to be a part of it. I started by helping out at public events or at the kennel where the dogs stay during the week. I ended up being Jed's puppy raiser when his became ill." Looking down at Jed, she says, "I'm really proud of this guy."

"He's a favorite around the station. Mark has to constantly remind us that he is working, just like we are."

"Jed's easy to love," Haley replies.

"And what about Mark?" Greg asks.

"He's easy to love too," Haley says and then asks, "Am I passing the test?"

"What test?" Greg says.

"If I was Mark's best friend, I'd be checking me out too. Here's this woman you know nothing about appearing in his life. I would imagine, considering everything Mark's gone through, that you would be protective of him."

"OK, you caught me. I admit it," Greg says.

"Let me tell you what you want to know. I will never hurt Mark. I just hope he doesn't hurt me."

By this time, the horseshoe game is over, and I return to Haley's side. I take Jed's leash and put my arm around her. "Greg isn't giving you a hard time, is he? Or filling your ear with his cop stories?"

"Right, don't get him started on his stories, Haley," Greg quickly responds.

"Hey, don't you have something better to do? Shouldn't you be going around refilling drinks like a good host?" I ask.

"Haley, if he starts getting on your nerves, just let me know. I'll straighten him out for you," Greg says as he walks away.

I give Haley a quick hug. I realize that I'm having fun and that she and Jed deserve most of the credit. I look out at all my fellow troopers and friends. I didn't often accept it, but so many of them offered help and support after the accident. I say a silent "thank you" to all of them, including Haley and Jed. Each of them has taught me about giving, and I feel like I've become a better version of my old self because of it.

Standing over the sink, scrubbing the grill grates is just the kind of job that allows my mind to wander while accomplishing something. I have never known time to pass so quickly. It seems like yesterday that Haley and I were making plans for the summer, and now it's August. It's hard for me to put into words the excitement and contentment I've felt having her here. I never realized how lonely and isolated I'd become until she entered my life. She's leaving in four days, and I don't know what I will do without her.

I was disappointed that MJ couldn't visit this summer. I was really looking forward to his meeting with Haley. I can just imagine the three of us having a great time together. But there will be other opportunities for this to happen. Right now, med school is his priority.

I can't believe how comfortably Haley and I fit together. It's been a long time since I've loved a woman. Haley is easy to love. I'm lucky to have found her, and I don't want us to go back to just weekends. I want her here beside me every day. I want her kiss in the morning and her greetings after work. I want to share my evenings with her and my bed.

We haven't talked about her leaving. I guess I keep trying to ignore the fact that it's going to happen. Would she stay if I asked her? Would she give up her old life to start a new one here with me? Maybe she wants me to quit my job and move out there with her? Either way I look at it, one of us has to make the bigger sacrifice. What can I offer her to stay here? All I have is myself, and I don't think I'm enough.

She interrupts my thoughts and my chore as she enters the kitchen. It is early evening, and she is out watering the flowers she planted. At the beginning of the summer, she asked if she could plant some annuals around the house. It made me laugh when she explained it would make the house look happy. Throughout the summer, as I watched her tend them, I realized that it made her happy too.

"Did you lose any flowers to the rabbits again?" I ask.

"Nope. All is well. You do realize, don't you, that you will have to take over the watering and weeding when I'm not here?" she explains.

"I'm trying not to think about it," I quickly answer.

"You're trying not to think about having to water or my leaving?" she questions me.

I give her a smirk and say, "Do you even have to ask?"

"It's nice to hear," she responds.

I take her hand and draw her over to me. I wrap my arms around her and say what has been on my mind for a long time now. "I don't want you to go. Stay here with me. Live with me."

Haley looks up at me. Neither one of us is saying anything. After a brief pause, she says, "Marry me."

I drop my arms from around her and lean back against the counter. It registers that all the times I have thought about us, I have never considered marriage. How can I explain my feelings without driving her away? I try my best to answer her.

"I love you, and I want to be with you. But every time I think of marriage, I think of bad stuff. I know it wasn't the same for you, but I don't ever want to go through that experience again."

"That was because you were never married to me," she says.

"What we have now is better than any marriage I know," I respond.

"We can be better than any marriage you know," she says. "I know it. I feel it. You can't be afraid to take a chance on me and what we have together."

"What's the difference if we have a piece of paper or not?" I add.

"The difference is you standing up before MJ and all your relatives and friends and declaring your love for me and pledging your life to me. It's your promise of a commitment that we will be together for the rest of our lives."

"I am committed to you for the rest of my life. That I am sure of."

"You're asking me to give up my job, my retirement, my home, and my friends and move out here with you, but you won't marry me? That doesn't seem like a commitment to me."

She takes a few steps backward to put space between us before she continues. "Would I do that for you? Yes, I love you. I want to spend the rest of my life with you."

I start toward her to bridge the space between us. She puts her hand out to stop me, and I step back to the counter.

"I know I would have to be the one to move," she says. "Your doctors are here, and your job is too. I can teach anywhere, and if there are no jobs, I can sub or tutor. But I need to know that you are in this relationship all the way with me. To me, that means marriage."

How do I make her understand how tainted I still am from my first marriage? I know Haley isn't anything like Melissa, but the damage has been done. "When we first met, I told you I didn't ever want to marry again," I remind her.

"I remember," Haley says. "But I wasn't in love with you then, and you weren't in love with me. Things change."

"Some things don't," I say, and I can see that these words hurt her more than anything else I've said.

The silence between us engulfs the kitchen. The emotions we are both feeling resonate around the room. I feel sick at how this has all played out. I bridge the gap between us, and this time she doesn't stop me. I take her hand and draw her to me. She reluctantly lets me pull her into my arms.

"Let's let it go for now. I'll be miserable if you are upset with me. Come to bed?" I ask.

I hold her hand as she follows me up the stairs. It reminds me of the first time we made love, except that now our positions are reversed. Things will work out, I tell myself. I know they will. We are both too emotional right now. We love each other. I believe in us.

CHAPTER 30

HALEY DUNCAN

I t was a long, restless night. The dogs must have picked up on our emotions because they couldn't seem to settle down. No one got much sleep.

Mark and Jed left for work earlier than normal, and I didn't bother to get up with them. I just stayed in bed, replaying last night over and over in my mind, each time hoping for a different result. It's like one of those sad movies I like to watch. Every time I watch it, I hope it will end differently, although I know it won't.

Mark hurt me deeply. When I moved in for the summer, it was to see what would become of our relationship. I guess it's my fault. I should have made it clear early on that marriage was always the end result for me. I didn't take him seriously when he said he would never marry again. I always felt that when the right woman came along, that would change. I thought I was that woman.

For the first time since I met Mark, I wonder what we really have as a couple. How could something that felt so right not end happily? Right now, I feel like I'm at a crossroads, and I don't know where I'm headed. But I do know that it's time for me to go home. What difference will three more days make? I need space and time to think about everything that's happened. I can't do that here, surrounded by everything that is him.

I get up and start packing. I'm surprised at how many things I've accumulated while I've been here. I try to do this quickly so the memories don't slow me down. Since I made my decision to leave, it feels like I can't be gone fast enough. I load up the car and sit down to compose the letter I will leave for Mark. I spend the rest of the morning collecting my thoughts and putting them down on paper.

> *Mark,*
>
> *Last night didn't work out as either of us hoped it would. I can't see a compromise to this situation, so in the end, one of us will have to change. I don't want to pressure you in any way, and I don't want to feel pressure from you, either. That's why I'm leaving today. I need time and space by myself to think. So do you. I have tried not to bring Jack into our relationship. He is my past. I had hoped that you would do the same with Melissa. She belongs to your past too. When I met you, I felt like we were both starting over. I never wanted our relationship to be defined by our past loves.*
>
> *Living together was never an arrangement that I was comfortable with. But because of the distance, it was the only way we could get to know each other. We are good together. I feel it, and I know you do too. When I look at my future, I can't imagine you not being a part of it. But I don't know if I can compromise on marriage. I want the fairy tale.*
>
> *Love,*
> *Haley*

I find myself sitting in my car, ready to leave and not able to turn the key. The dogs are in the back, and everything is packed up and ready to go. I've left the letter sitting on the kitchen table, where Mark will find it easily. As I sit here, I realize how wrong this is. I thought I could just drive away, but I realize I can't do that. It's not fair to Mark to leave in this manner. I would hate it if I came home and found him gone. I need to stay and say goodbye in person. The letter can explain the rest.

I get the dogs out of the car, and they look at me in puzzlement. They know something is up and are reluctant to leave my side. I realize it is past lunchtime, so I head for the kitchen. I'm not hungry, but I make myself eat some fruit and nibble on some crackers. I feel at a loss, and I don't know what to do with myself. I have never had trouble keeping myself busy while Mark was at work before, but today the afternoon stretches on endlessly.

I finally decide to take the dogs to the neighborhood park. As I pull into the parking lot, I realize that it hurts to be here. This place is full of great memories of the five of us. I wonder if this will be our last visit. The dogs are already heading down the path to the woods. They know the way and lead me with their boundless enthusiasm. I can't catch their energy today nor enjoy the beauty of the park. The trails are shaded and cool, and I walk until the dogs are tired and thirsty, and it's time to start back.

As I pull into Mark's driveway, I stop and look at the house I've called home for the summer. I remember the first time I came and the excitement I felt. A lot has happened in those ten months. I shake the memories away and take the dogs around back for some water. They follow me into the house and stay with me as I wander from room to room. I stop in the living room and gaze at the painting on the fireplace mantle. I remember vividly the day I gave it to Mark. I look down at my bracelet and trace the two silver bands. Our lives are intertwined, but maybe our futures are not.

The dogs and I go out front and take up Mark and Jed's spot on the porch. I think about all the time Mark spent waiting here to welcome me and how symbolic it is that I am the one waiting here now to say goodbye.

Finally, I see the bus pulling in at the stop at the end of the circle. Mark and Jed get off, and I notice that Mark has flowers in his hand. As they walk home, Brandon comes running out of his house to meet them. I can't stop a small grimace as I see Alexandra following close behind him. She is smiling and flirty as I watch the three of them talk. I can't help but wonder what is being said. As Mark turns and heads home, I realize that he won't have to look far for companionship if I'm not around. When Mark sees us sitting on the porch, he releases Jed from his leash and allows him to greet us. Jed runs to me for a quick hello, and then his attention goes to Magic and Thunder. To watch them, you would think they haven't seen each other in years.

Mark hands me the flowers. "For you," he says. "Nothing went right today because we're not right. I know I've disappointed you. I feel like I've let you down. Let's forget last night ever happened and just go on as we've been."

We stand facing each other, not touching. "The flowers are beautiful. Thank you." After a pause, I say, "Last night happened, and it needed to. At some point, we had to talk about the future." Looking up into his troubled eyes, I manage to keep it together as I let him know I'm leaving. "I need time to think about us, and so do you. I can't do that here. So I'm going home today, but I didn't want to leave without saying goodbye. I left you a letter on the kitchen table. I tried to put into words what I'm thinking."

Mark doesn't say anything but continues to look at me. His eyes are guarded now. I feel awful. This really hurts. I put the dogs and flowers in the car and turn and give Jed a hug. When I look back at Mark, I can feel my eyes starting to tear.

"I love you, but I feel we need some time apart. I'll text when I get home like I always do."

Mark is still not saying anything. I can feel him distancing himself from me already. I quickly hug him, but I don't feel him return it. I step back and look at him, and it strikes me that this could be the end for us.

I get in the car and start the engine. Mark and Jed are standing side-by-side, watching as I pull out of the driveway. I look in the rearview mirror before I turn the corner, and I see that they are already walking up the sidewalk toward the house. My breath catches as I realize they look just like the painting.

CHAPTER 31

MARK LANCER

These last few days have been rainy, which suits my mood perfectly. It's been over a week since Haley left, and nothing seems to be going right. I knew the start of her school year was quickly approaching, and I was preparing myself for her leaving. I just never imagined it would be this kind of goodbye. If I had just kept my mouth shut, nothing would have been said, and nothing would have changed.

Looking out the bus window on my way to work, I think about last night. On my way home, Brandon came running out with his ball and glove. "Officer Mark, can you play catch with me?"

He is hard to resist, so I put Jed in a down/stay, and we tossed the ball back and forth.

"How's school going?" I asked.

"Good. Miss Douglas is my teacher, and she's really nice."

"Most teachers are," I replied, thinking of Haley.

Alexandra appeared at the front door. "Brandon, it's time for supper."

"I can't, Mom. I'm playing catch with Officer Mark," he replied.

"I'm sure Officer Mark has to eat supper, too," she said. "You're welcome to join us, Mark. We're having spaghetti, and there is always plenty."

"Please, Officer Mark, that would be so cool," Brandon begged.

Looking from mother to son and feeling the way I do, I decide to take them up on their offer. "Spaghetti is one of my favorite meals," I replied.

"Brandon, lead the way," Alexandra said.

Brandon led me into the house, saying, "Mom, I'm showing Officer Mark and Jed my room."

She looked at me, smiling. "OK, I'll have dinner ready when you two finish."

Brandon's room reminded me of MJ's at that age. Posters of his heroes were on the wall, and his bedspread looked like a baseball diamond. As we went downstairs, the smell of the spaghetti led us into the dining room, where Alexandra was waiting. We enjoyed a pleasant meal together, with Brandon dominating most of the conversation.

"Last week, you had flowers. Were those for Miss Haley?" he asked.

"Yes, they were," I answered.

"Did she go back home yesterday?" Alexandra asked.

"Her school is almost ready to start," I responded.

"I'm sorry, but I couldn't help but notice when I was out getting the mail that it didn't seem like a happy goodbye," Alexandra said.

"We'll work it out," I said, and after a moment, I asked, "Would you ever consider marrying again?"

"I'm not the best person to ask. I've been divorced twice so far," she responded.

"Twice?" I repeated.

"The first was my college sweetheart. We got married right out of school because that seemed like the thing to do. When we joined the real world, we found out we had little in common and very different goals. It was a mutual decision and an amicable divorce. Brandon's father was another story. He had a case of the roaming eye."

"What's the roaming eye?" Brandon asked his mother.

"You'll learn about that when you're older, Brandon," she answered.

"It was a messy divorce, and we're still fighting about it. He's living with his secretary now."

"Would you ever consider marrying for the third time?" I asked.

"I would probably prefer living together," she responded. "But then again, I would have to consider Brandon and the man's wishes."

"I think there's a lot to be said for living together," I said.

"I'm all for it, but I'm getting the impression that Haley isn't," Alexandra said.

"It's a point of discussion between us," I replied.

"Make sure you stay true to yourself. I've found out that doing things to make the other person happy rarely works out," she added.

"We'll work out," I said.

After dinner, when I was saying goodbye, Alexandra said, "You know where I am if you need someone to talk to or just some good company."

I just nodded and turned with Jed to go home. Even though it was a perfectly innocent dinner, I felt like I stepped out of bounds. I would never do anything to hurt Haley, but I feel if she knew about this dinner, I would have done just that.

As I get off the bus and head into my workplace, I put those thoughts aside. This is bad timing to have my personal life in a mess. Tomorrow we are staging an ammunition bust that the station has been working on for over a year. With the help of the Feds, we hope to dismantle a major weapons trafficking network. I've been working behind the scenes on this from the beginning, and I can't get distracted now.

I've been eating lunch at my desk all week. Not because I was so busy with the raid but because I just didn't feel like dealing with anybody. Today I force myself to take a break and go to the lunchroom. On entering, I see Greg sitting by himself at one of the tables by the window. I go over and join him.

"Hey, how's it going?" he says.

"It's going. How about you?"

"I'm ready to get these scumbag gunrunners."

"Me too. It's been a year of undercover work, and it all comes down to tomorrow night," I add.

"You orchestrated most of the plan. Do you think we'll get the ring leaders?"

"I'm pretty confident with the plan we put together. If everyone executes properly, the whole operation will come down. We just have to be prepared for the unexpected."

"If this operation is a success, you deserve a lot of the credit," Greg says. "You've been a big part of trying to get these weapons off the streets." After a pause, he asks, "So, how's Haley doing?"

"She left," I answer.

"I know she left. It's after Labor Day. All schools are back in session," he responds.

"No, she left, *left!*" I say.

"What do you mean she left, *left?*" he asks.

"I asked her to stay and move in with me. She wants me to marry her," I say, shaking my head.

"I hope you said yes," he quickly replies.

"I didn't. You know how ugly my divorce from Melissa was. I swore I would never marry again. I told Haley that when we first met. I don't see why we can't just live together. Everybody lives together in this day and age. What we have is just about perfect."

"For you, it was perfect, but what about for her?" Greg asks.

"She was happy. I know she was. We were both happy," I respond.

"Haley is the marrying kind. I can see that from what little I know of her. You two seemed perfect together."

"I thought we were. I don't know why this has to be so complicated."

"It's not. You're just making it that way by carrying your divorce into this relationship. Marry her. Start over. Give yourself a new life."

"Sure, and how do I say, 'Marry me. I want to be with you forever. Oh, by the way, I want you to sign this prenup'?"

"Is that the problem?" Greg asks, surprised.

"It's just one of them," I answer.

"Has it ever occurred to you that she might want one herself? Listen, I know you. We've been friends for a long time. Sitting down and having a heart-to-heart with someone is not one of your strong points. But you have to make this right with Haley, or I have a feeling you are going to regret it for the rest of your life."

"That's easy for you to say. You're a happily married man. You've never been in an unhappy marriage, and you've never been divorced."

"I'm sure there are plenty of unhappy, divorced men out there who would jump at the chance to marry Haley," Greg answers.

I just glare at him, gather up my tray, and get up to leave. "I have to get back to work."

"Hey, I'm on your side, you know," Greg calls after me as I walk away.

I leave the lunchroom, wishing I had just stayed at my desk.

CHAPTER 32

HALEY DUNCAN

❝ Not much to tell here, Cassie. School is going well. I have a good schedule this year, and so far, I like all my classes."

"Haley, I can hear your pain three states away," Cassie says.

"I doubt that," I respond.

"This affair of yours had heartbreak written all over it from the beginning. You're usually so perceptive about people and so good at guarding your heart. What happened?"

"Jed happened, and then Mark happened," I answer.

"Have you heard from Mark?"

"We keep in touch a couple of times a week."

"Is that a smart thing to do?"

"I don't know, but for now, it feels right."

"How long since you've seen him?"

"It's been a month now. He asked me to visit last weekend, but I didn't think anything had changed, so I didn't. I don't know what more there is to say. After all, he did tell me when I first met him that he would never marry again."

"If he won't marry you, you need to make a clean break of it, Haley."

"I don't think I'm there yet. Mark just needs time to sort things out. He has a lot of baggage from his first marriage."

"That has nothing to do with you."

"I know, but I've never been divorced, so I don't know what it's like. But I believe in us. It's just painful disagreeing about this."

"I think it's more painful for you than him!"

"I'm sure that's not true. It affects both of us and even the dogs. Last weekend, I went out to the garage, and I accidentally left the door open. Of course, Magic and Thunder came barreling out of the house. To my great surprise, instead of taking off into the neighborhood, they both ran to the car and sat looking at me and waiting. They know the routine, and they were ready to go visit Jed. It's not like I can explain it to them."

"Haley, they're dogs."

"They are more perceptive than most people I know. How is it that I'm the only one in the family that ended up with the dog gene?"

"Don't ask me where your love for animals came from. It bypassed the rest of us. Anyway, you're changing the subject again, which you're so good at."

"Listen, Cassie. I'm doing the best I can."

"I just hate to see you hurt again."

"I'm fine, honestly. I'm just waiting for Mark to sort this out."

"Promise me you'll make a clean break if he doesn't come around. Find someone who's worthy of your love."

"I thought I did."

"If I ever get to meet him, I'm going to give him a piece of my mind."

"You would like him, Cassie."

"I'm not so sure about that."

"Listen, I know what I'm doing. If I decide to break off all contact with Mark, I will. But it will be on my own timing."

"I'm always in your corner, Haley. You know that. You've had enough pain to last a lifetime already."

"He brought me a lot of happiness too."

"So, you think it equals out?"

"I don't know. This isn't over yet."

"You need to think about what's best for you."

"Spoken like a true sister."

I shake my head as I end the call. I could have done without that discussion. I know Cassie means well, but I could use a cheerleader instead of a doomsayer. I look over at Magic and Thunder lounging on the floor. Thank goodness for my dogs. They never let me down.

CHAPTER 33

MARK LANCER

❝ MJ, I'm glad you called."

"It's called FaceTime, Dad, and you look tired."

"It must be your phone. You look great," I respond. "How's school?"

"Hard. They say the second year of med school is the worst of the four."

"Who is 'they'?" I ask.

"'They' is everybody I know who has survived it."

"I have full faith and confidence in you."

"I hope you can say that at the end of this year. That's when I have to take my first board test. Everyone's talking about it already."

"Are you having doubts?"

"You know everyone here is incredibly bright. It's easy to question myself and wonder if I'm good enough."

"There is no question that you're good enough. You had your choice of three medical schools."

"So did a lot of other people here."

"You're not like other people."

"Spoken like a true father."

"I know my son."

"How's your work going?"

"That's going really well. I'm sure it didn't make the California news, but we just orchestrated a major weapons trafficking bust. It took us a year of undercover investigation to learn that Pittsburgh is one of the hubs for illegal gun distribution. Those guns won't be flowing through our city again any time soon. We got lucky. Not only did we take down the organization, but we nailed all the kingpins too."

"Another victory for the good guys! Was it your plan?" MJ asks.

"I had some input," I reply.

"I'm sure it was more than some."

"Anyway, it felt good."

"You don't sound like things are good. How are you doing since Haley left?"

"It's OK."

"It doesn't sound OK. You should have asked her to stay."

"I did."

"Way to go! What'd she say?"

"She asked me to marry her."

"Awesome! She asked you! That takes all the pressure off."

"It's not awesome. You know the bad experience I had with your mother."

"That was ages ago with Mom."

"That was not ages ago. Anyway, when I first met Haley, I told her I didn't plan on ever getting married again."

"Dad, all men say that after a bad divorce. Come on. You got lucky to find this wonderful woman who you're crazy about. Why wouldn't you want to commit to her? That makes no sense to me! What are you afraid of?"

"I'm not afraid."

"Yes, you are. I hate to say this, but she has more to lose by marrying you than you do."

"You don't understand."

"Wait, hear me out. She's the one who would probably have to move because it would be a lot harder for you to get another job with your history of seizures. She would have to quit her job, sell her home, leave her friends, and start all over again with you."

"Not necessarily," I quickly respond, even though I know he's right.

"Dad, you know I'm right."

"OK, I know. Haley said the same thing."

"What would you be giving up for her?" MJ says, knowing full well that I don't have an answer. "Marrying her seems like nothing compared to what she's willing to do for you. You should be down on your knees begging her to marry you."

"You haven't even met her yet."

"I feel like I have. I have a good feeling about her. She has to be caring to be a teacher, and she has to be compassionate to have raised Jed. To do both of those things, she has to have a lot of patience, which she needs when you get quiet and stubborn."

"I don't get quiet and stubborn."

"Hey, this is me you're talking to. Once upon a time, I lived with you."

"That was then. I'm different now."

"And Haley had a lot to do with that. I've seen the change in you since you met her. I don't ever remember you being as happy as you've been this last year. Don't make a big mistake here, Dad."

"You're not making me feel any better about all of this, MJ."

"Are you and Haley still talking?"

"We still text and email. I haven't seen her since she left at the end of August. I asked her to visit this weekend, but she declined. I think she is slowly breaking up with me."

"You can fix this, Dad."

"I'm not sure I can," I reply.

"I'm sure you can. Marry her and let yourself start over."

"OK, MJ, enough advice for one day."

"I want you to be happy. I hate thinking of you alone."

"I'm not alone. I have Jed."

"Dad!"

"I know. Change is hard for me. It's hard for me to trust women after your mother."

"It doesn't sound like Haley's anything like Mom."

"She is nothing like your mother."

"Then quit comparing them. Go for it. Remember what you always tell me about life being too short."

"I know I'm the problem here. I just have to wrap my head around the idea of getting married again. I know the next move is mine."

"I'm with you all the way, Dad."

"I know, MJ. Quit worrying about me. I plan on working this out with Haley."

"I hope so."

"Take care of yourself, and thanks."

"For what?"

"Just thanks."

Still looking at my phone after the call is over, I realize that without meeting Haley, I have MJ's blessing. I wonder if I will be as open-minded when he brings a woman home.

Chapter 34

Emails

From: Mark Lancer
To: Haley Duncan
Subject: Important
Haley,
It seems like a lifetime since I've seen you. I miss you. I miss us. We have both had plenty of time to think by now. Although I have hated every minute of us being apart, it gave me time to do some soul-searching. For me, this was needed and way overdue. I am ready to talk about us, but I don't want to do it by phone or Facetime. I have some explaining to do. Please let me see you. Also, I have something to give you, and I want to do it face-to-face. If you won't come here, then let me come there. I will make the trip whenever it suits you. I love you, Haley.
Mark

––––––––––––––––––––––––––

From: Haley Duncan
To: Mark Lancer
Subject: OK
Mark,
I've been struggling with all sorts of feelings and emotions since I left you. This hasn't been easy. I do agree that it's time we get together and talk. I also have been doing some soul-searching and have things I need to say to you. I will come there. It's just easier that way. I'll come on a Saturday like I did at the very beginning. This weekend is homecoming, and I've agreed to chaperone some of the school activities, so we will have to wait until the following Saturday. Let me know if this works for you. I love you too.
Haley

————————————————————

To: Haley Duncan
From: Mark Lancer
Subject: Thank you
Haley,
Thank you for agreeing to come. Jed and I will be waiting, like always, for you next Saturday. I can't wait to see you.
Mark

————————————————————

To: Mark Lancer
From: Haley Duncan
Subject: Me too
Mark,
It's a plan. The three of us will be there next Saturday around noon. I miss you too.
Haley

CHAPTER 35

STATE CAPITAL AWARDS CEREMONY

❝ This morning, as Pennsylvania's governor, I would like to
acknowledge the incredible work our state police force did
helping the Bureau of Alcohol, Tobacco, Firearms, and
Explosives with their recent weapons bust. Over a year of investigative
work on this case culminated successfully two weeks ago. The two
forces working cooperatively were able to shut down a major gun
trafficking network that operated in this area. The number and types
of weaponry found were shocking. Now those firearms will never hit
our streets. Sergeant Dean, as governor of this great state, I would
like to personally thank you and your force for a job well done."

Shaking the governor's hand, Sergeant Dean steps up to the
microphone. "Thank you, Governor, and I promise to keep my
remarks short. A trooper's job is difficult and isolating. The rotating
shifts make it hard on the officer's social and family life. We work
twenty-four hours a day, three hundred sixty-five days a year. There
are emergencies requiring us to drop everything we are doing and
report for duty. We may have to miss birthday parties, kids' sporting
events, anniversaries, and even vacations. This is the reality of our
job, and we are all willing to do it to keep our communities safe.

"People have a tendency to forget that our work is spent mostly with the bad part of society. We meet all types of people, see all kinds of environments, and are put in all kinds of different situations. We can spend the morning at a mansion and the afternoon at a trash dump. The stress we experience is unique and different from other jobs. In seconds, we might have to react to an out-of-control situation that could mean life or death. This makes burnout an occupational hazard in our line of work. I have seen it end the careers of a lot of good officers.

"The absolute worst part of our job is when we have to notify family or next of kin that a loved one has died. Even years later, police officers can still see the faces of the mothers, fathers, husbands, wives, and children as they broke the terrible news. These people won't forget what was said and how we said it for the rest of their lives. It is an extremely stressful and exhausting part of the job.

"My men and I are proud to serve this great state. My officers put their lives on the line every day. We are pleased this operation ended without loss of life and the kingpins are now in custody. We appreciate the state acknowledging our work. This award goes to the men under my command. Each one of them had a part in making it a success. In closing, I would like to thank the governor, the bureau, the task force, and all the officers who were involved. Chalk one up for the good guys."

As Sergeant Dean returns to his seat in the capitol rotunda, he receives a text from his second in command. There has been an explosion at the police station. Many are wounded, some critically. Giving an abrupt wave to the governor, he is out the door. With the siren blaring, he makes the fifteen-minute ride back to the station. Along the way, a chorus of other sirens from medical emergency vehicles and fire engines can be heard.

Approaching the scene, the air smells of smoke and burning. Most of the back part of the station is gone. Debris is scattered everywhere. There are pieces of twisted metal and brick on the sidewalk where some of his officers are getting medical attention. Others have already been taken away in ambulances to nearby hospitals.

Standing in the midst of the destruction, Sergeant Dean starts to register what has happened here. The horror is only beginning.

CHAPTER 36

HALEY DUNCAN

Wednesday started out just like any other day. As a schoolteacher, I am prepared for every day to be different. It is one of the many things I enjoy about teaching. Looking back, there should have been some warning or indication that today was going to be unlike any other. My life would change today. My future would change today.

Without knocking, Principal Richards walks into my room during my fourth-period class. He surprises me with his visit, but one look at his face and I know it isn't good. He turns his back to the class and says quietly, "Haley, you need to go to the office and take a phone call. This can't wait. I'll stay here and cover your class for you."

This is not the standard procedure for phone calls. Normally, if a call comes during class, the secretaries take a message and have us return the call when we're free. I feel immediate dread.

"Is there a problem?" I ask.

He just shakes his head and says, "Go, now. Don't keep him waiting."

I can feel my heart beating in my chest as I hurriedly walk to the office. My mind is racing in all different directions. Did something happen to Mom or Dad or Cassie or her family? Maybe something happened at my home? Oh please, let my dogs be all right. By the time I near the office, I am panicked. I want to find out what's going on, yet I don't. Once you know, you can never go back. I try to calm myself.

"Relax, Haley. Stop and catch your breath. Who says this is going to be something terrible? It could be something wonderful, like being nominated Teacher of the Year."

Shaking my head at myself, I take a few breaths as I open the office door. When I approach the counter, Julie, the main secretary, tells me to take the call in the small meeting room.

"So you have privacy," she says.

I am about to ask her who is calling, but her eyes quickly look away, and I get the message. I was right. This isn't good. I enter the small room and sit down by the phone. I take another deep breath and pick it up.

"Hello. This is Haley Duncan."

"Haley, this is Sergeant Dean of the Pennsylvania State Police. We met last summer at Greg Dobler's Fourth of July picnic."

"Yes, I remember. You're Mark's sergeant."

"I am sorry to inform you that we have experienced a situation here. There has been an explosion at our station house, and we are dealing with multiple injuries and possible casualties."

"Oh no," I gasp. "Is Mark all right?"

"All I can tell you right now is that his service dog has been badly injured, and your name is listed as the emergency contact. The dog is being transported to the local animal hospital, where we take our police dogs. They need you to contact them as soon as possible so they have permission to treat the animal. The number is 219-702-6205."

"Wait, let me write it down."

There is a pad and pen sitting by the phone that I grab. My hand is shaking as I write the number down. I feel like I've been ambushed from both sides. If Jed is hurt, Mark must be too.

"Please, I know Mark must be hurt for you to call me about Jed. Can't you tell me how he is?"

"I am sorry, Haley, but I am not at liberty to disclose any information at this time. If I could, it would only be with the immediate family."

And there it is. I'm not family to Mark under the law.

"I'll be leaving immediately to come out there. I know I'm not family, but Mark and I have been together for over a year," I plead.

"I'm sorry, Haley, but it's not my call. That will be up to the immediate family."

"Can't you tell me anything?" I ask frantically.

"Watch the news. The press usually manages to find out these things before they should," he responds sympathetically.

"I understand," I manage to say.

"Haley, take good care of his dog. Trooper Lancer loves that dog. We all do here."

"I will."

I don't even manage to say goodbye. I've been gripping the phone so tight that my fingers are cramped when I put the receiver down. I get up and pace the room to try to catch my breath and stop the pounding in my heart.

"Jed, I have to take care of Jed. Don't think of anything else right now," I tell the empty room.

I sit back down and put the call through to the school switchboard. After what seems like an eternity, I'm finally connected.

"City Line Animal Hospital. Can you hold?"

"No, I can't hold. Jed, a service dog, was brought into your clinic from the explosion at the state police headquarters. I need to OK treatment!"

"Oh yes, let me page you through to Dr. Stevens."

I panic that I will be put on hold or that my call will go through to voice mail, but almost immediately, I hear a deep voice on the line.

"Is this Haley Duncan?"

"Yes, it is. How is Jed?"

"He is responsive but needs immediate surgery. His front leg is badly mangled, and he may lose it. He's also lost a lot of blood. But of what I'm hearing on the news, he is better off than most."

"Are you equipped to do the surgery there?" I ask.

"Yes, and I will be performing it as soon as I have your consent," he responds.

"You have it. Please take good care of him. He is a valuable service dog. Do everything you can to save his leg."

"I plan to," he responds.

"I live four hours away, but I will get there as soon as possible. Is there anything you can tell me about the explosion?"

"Not much. They are talking about a bomb with possible dead and many injured," he informs me.

This information is shocking to me. "A bomb at the police station? That is hard to believe!"

"It is, isn't it?" he replies. "Sorry, but I must go. They are prepping Jed now."

"Please take good care of him," I plead.

"I will do my best," he replies.

As I hang up the phone, my mind is already organizing everything I have to do before I can leave. I race out of the office and back to my classroom. I meet up with Principal Richards on the way.

"I have arranged coverage for you for the rest of the day. I figured you would be leaving immediately," he gently says. "Is it all bad news?"

"There's been an explosion," I reply.

"I'm aware. I heard it on the news."

"Jed, the service dog I raised, is headed to surgery right now. They won't tell me anything about Mark, his owner."

"Go, but keep me up-to-date on what's happening," he says.

"I will," I manage to get out as I head to my classroom.

"Haley," he calls after me. I turn back and look at him. "I'll hope for the best."

I can hear the sincerity in his words. "Thank you," I say and manage a weak smile. Then I turn and race to my room just as classes are changing.

Luckily, I have lunch duty next, so I can quickly write some plans for the rest of the day without my students bombarding me with questions. I arrange the afternoon assignments on my desk, grab my purse and laptop, and rush out the door.

In the fifteen minutes that it takes me to drive home, I arrange for my dog sitter to come and take care of Magic and Thunder. I don't know what to tell her when she asks how long I will be gone.

She is wonderful, as usual, telling me not to worry and to take all the time I need.

When I arrive home, I see Magic and Thunder sleeping by the front window. Dogs are creatures of habit, so I surprise them when I pull into the driveway. They are used to my school schedule, and this is definitely not the usual time I get home. Despite the interruption of their nap time, they are overjoyed to see me. I give them each a snack, hug them tightly, and head to the bedroom. I start throwing some clothes into my travel sack, realizing I have no idea what I might need. I quickly figure that three of everything should be enough to get me into the weekend. This gives me focus, and I remind myself that if I need anything else, I can just buy it there. Within minutes, I am packed. I gather up my toiletries, grab my laptop, and head for the door. Magic and Thunder are both watching me with wary eyes. I stop and give them both hugs.

"Jed is hurt. I have to go and make sure he's OK. You guys be good while I'm gone."

As I pull out of the driveway, I wonder if I can hold it together for the next four hours. I know something bad has happened to Mark, or else I wouldn't have been contacted about Jed. But how bad is it? That is what I need to know. Let him be all right. He's had enough tragedy in his life already. Let this one pass him by.

While I drive, I flip through the channels on the radio for news of the explosion. Most of the reports I hear do not tell me anything new, but by the end of the first hour of my trip, the news is definitely more specific.

"A bomb is reported to have caused the explosion at the Hill Street Police Station House. It was strategically planted at the back of the building, where it would affect the most people. All of the injured have been transported to area hospitals. No one is verifying it, but we believe there have been casualties. Stay tuned for further updates."

By the end of my second hour of travel, law enforcement finally breaks its silence and holds a press conference. I hear Sergeant Dean's voice coming through my radio.

"I would like to read a brief statement. I will not accept any questions at this time. At 9:42 this morning, there was an explosion at the state police headquarters on Hill Street. It originated near the back of the station house. So far, we have determined that it was a powerful explosive device. This was not an accident. The criminals who are responsible for this were extremely knowledgeable about explosives. Troopers and office personnel working in the building were injured by the blast, some critically. As of last count, nineteen have been transported to local hospitals. We expect some fatalities. No more information will be released about injured personnel until the families and next of kin are notified. Please keep the injured and their families in your thoughts at this difficult time. In the days and weeks to come, we will get to the bottom of this assault and bring the perpetrators to justice. If anyone has any information concerning this incident, please call the hotline at 1-800-777-6541. Thank you."

During my third hour of driving, news personnel are trying to guess the perpetrators of the bombing. Their ideas range from a vendetta against the law enforcement community to a retaliatory strike because of a recent major weapons bust. Never once do they mention a terrorist attack, so that option must have no merit.

I can't take listening anymore. I turn off the radio and drive the rest of the way in silence. It occurs to me that I've never made this trip alone before. Magic and Thunder have always kept me company. How I wish they were with me now. Finally, I enter the city limits with no idea what is ahead of me.

As I pull into the City Line Animal Hospital, I realize that I recognize the place. When Mark gave me his city tour, he pointed out that this is where he brings Jed. After finding a place to park, I rush into the building. I make my way through the busy waiting room to the receptionist.

"Can you please help me? I'm Haley Duncan, and I'm here for Jed, the service dog who was injured in the explosion. Please, can you tell me how he's doing? I have to make sure Jed is OK, and then I somehow have to find out how his owner is doing."

"Oh yes, we've been waiting for you. Jed is out of surgery and in recovery. Follow me, and Dr. Stevens will talk to you as soon as possible." I follow her down the hallway to what turns out to be Dr. Stevens's office. "Take a seat, and I will let him know you are here."

"Thank you," I reply.

I don't sit. I pace. I have been sitting for four hours in uncertainty, and I have the urge to be moving. I remind myself that I need to keep all my fears and emotions in check until I know for sure what has happened. It couldn't have been more than a five-minute wait when Dr. Stevens enters his office. I search his face for clues, but he is unreadable.

"The surgery went well. I was able to save the leg, but the damage is extensive."

"Oh, thank goodness. What exactly does 'extensive' mean?"

"I believe his gait will never be perfect again, but in time, the leg should be able to bear weight and function. What that degree of function will be, we'll just have to wait and see."

"Can he walk?" I ask.

"I have a cast on the leg now. Jed will adapt while he is healing. The leg will need to be checked in two weeks. You can see him now if you wish, but he's sleeping off the anesthesia, so I wouldn't bother. I want him to stay here overnight, just as a precaution. If all goes well, you can probably take him home tomorrow. Do you have any other questions for me?"

"I need to see him, even if he's sleeping," I say.

"Very well, follow me."

I follow him back to what must be the recovery room. Jed is lying on his side on a blanket in a large dog run. It looks like they shaved half his body for the surgery. He has an IV in his left front leg, a tube providing oxygen in his mouth, and a cast on his right front leg. It brings me to tears just looking at him.

I turn to Dr. Stevens. He seems like a kind and caring doctor, and I'm glad that Jed is in his care. "I don't have any questions right now, but I'm sure I will," I say. "Thank you for saving his leg and letting me see him. I will come tomorrow morning to pick him up if you feel he is ready to be discharged. Right now, I have to go and find out about Mark Lancer, his owner."

"I hope he's as lucky as Jed," he replies. "I'll see you tomorrow."

I have to keep myself from running out of his office. I have been racking my brain trying to figure out how I can get information about Mark. If we were married, I wouldn't have this problem. Anger is mixing in with my fear right now. Who can I get to talk to me? I know the hospitals won't tell me anything because I'm not family. I'm sure the reporters are not releasing any personal information on the news. I don't even have a key to Mark's house. My only option is to find someone who knows me and beg for information. That means I have to go to the station house or what is left of it.

Mark's house is on my way, so I drive by just in case there is any activity there. Seeing none, I continue around the circle and head for the station. Because of the bombing, traffic is busier than normal, and it takes me twice as long to maneuver through it. As I get closer to the station, I can see that many of the streets are blocked off. I find a place to park a couple of blocks away and hurry to the scene.

The smell of the blast is still lingering in the air. I can definitely see that most of the damage is to the back of the building. I'm pretty sure I remember Mark telling me that he liked to park in the back because it was closer to his desk. I manage to make my way through the swarm of reporters and bystanders milling around. I am desperate to find someone who knows me, someone who will help me. I walk up and down behind the police tape, searching the police and bystanders. Finally, I see Greg Dobler, Mark's best friend, getting into his patrol car.

"Greg!" I yell as I race to his car.

"Haley. I was wondering if anyone contacted you," he says.

"The sergeant called me about Jed since Mark had me as a contact, but he wouldn't tell me anything about Mark. Please, I can't take this! I'm frantic! You have to tell me how he is and get me in to see him. Greg, Mark would want to see me. Please help me!"

I notice that Greg has broken off eye contact with me. When his eyes return to mine, I can read the anguish in them and on his face. Before he can say anything, I know. "He's dead, isn't he?" I manage to get out.

It seems like forever that he stands there looking at me before he gives me a slight nod of his head. "He and two others so far. I just can't believe it. It could have been any of us."

My hands cover my face as if this can block out his words.

"Mark was just too close to the explosion. From what medical personnel can tell so far, he was thrown by the blast and died instantly."

I feel physically sick at his words. I look up at him and see the anguish on his face that I'm sure mirrors my own. "Take me to see him," I say.

"Haley, that's not a good idea."

I shake my head frantically. "You have to take me. I can't bear not to see him again. I don't care what state he's in."

"Even if I wanted to, I'm not sure I can," he says.

"Please, Greg, you have to do this for me," I plead.

He continues to stare at me while he decides what to do. Finally, he simply motions with his head to his patrol car. I race around to the passenger side and get in.

We ride in silence. I don't pay any attention to where he's taking me. My eyes are dry, and right now, I feel like screaming loud and hard. I'm not sure I can bear this pain again. I try to calm myself as I look out the side window.

We turn in at the regional hospital, and Greg parks at the curb in the fire lane. As ridiculous as it seems at this moment, the thought strikes me that he is parking in an illegal parking spot. I shake my head, trying to clear out all the crazy things that I'm thinking. We both get out of the car at the same time, but I wait for him to take the lead as we enter the hospital.

Greg motions to some chairs in the waiting room. "Haley, wait here while I see what I can do."

The waiting room is crowded. As I find a vacant seat, I wonder if all these people are here for the same reason I am. I watch Greg as he approaches the nursing station and begins talking to one of the nurses on duty. It is amazing the power his uniform carries. In only a few minutes, he is back beside me.

"Mark is still here," he says. "They haven't moved him yet. Follow me, and you can see him for a few minutes."

"Thank you for doing this for me, Greg."

"They told me he looks OK. His injuries were mostly internal. His son has been notified and is on his way. They plan on keeping him here until MJ arrives."

Greg and I follow another nurse who is waiting for us. She leads us down a maze of hallways until she stops at one of the rooms. Then she turns and walks back in the direction we just came. I turn to Greg and ask, "Can I be alone with him?"

He nods. "I'll wait out here."

The room only has one bed, and Mark appears to be sleeping there. As I walk over to him, I realize that this is the last time I will ever be alone with him. I am tired of holding in all my emotions.

I've kept them under control for hours now, and I just can't do it anymore. I grab his bruised hand and hold it between both of mine. It surprises me that it is still warm to the touch. I can feel the tears running down my face and my eyes starting to burn.

In all the time I've been with Mark, I have never seen him still, even during sleep. His stillness now grabs at my heart. The reality of his death washes over me. I cradle his hand in mine and hold it tightly as if I can transfer some of my life into him. I stay like this for some time until I'm able to speak.

"I'm here. I hope, wherever you are, you know that. I love you. I hope you know that too."

I frantically wipe away my tears so I can continue to look at him.

"We were so good together. We would have made it. I know we would have. I wish I knew what you wanted to say to me and to give me. I wish so many things that won't happen now."

I pause, wanting to feel his eyes on me one more time.

"You know I'll take good care of Jed. His heart is going to be broken too."

I don't hear the quiet knock on the door, but I feel Greg's presence as he enters the room.

"Haley, it's time to go."

I touch Mark's face with my hand, trying to memorize the feel of him, trying to say goodbye. I kiss him gently on the forehead and then on the lips and whisper one last time to him. "You'll always be in my heart."

I kiss his hand and lower it back down to the sheet. I take a step back from the bed and look at him for the last time. It takes everything in me to back away from his side. Shattered, I turn and leave the hospital room.

CHAPTER 37

MJ LANCER

O nce a month, I have dinner with my mother. Being in the same city with her gives me little excuse not to do this. If I make sure this happens, then I don't have to listen to her complain.

"MJ, you hardly spent any time with me."

"Mom, I'm studying all the time, and you're working most of the time."

"That's just an excuse. If your dad lived here instead of me, you would see him on a regular basis," she says.

"Don't start that again," I reply.

"It's true, and you know it," she quickly adds.

I don't respond. What can I say to her? *You're right, Mom. Dad's never let me down.* I just keep walking. Tonight we are going to a pub near my apartment. Even though it is raining lightly, we are walking the four blocks. The sidewalk is busy with people, and Mom uses this as an excuse to link her arm through mine as we go.

"How's the shop?" I ask, intent on changing the subject.

"Business is great. You know, MJ, opening the boutique was just what I needed in my life."

"You sure didn't need Dad in your life."

"That's not fair. I have a right to be happy."

"I've never understood why you weren't happy."

"MJ, you have to let it go. It's been a long time now."

"It may seem that way to you, but it doesn't to me."

"That's because you've kept busy being mad at me."

"No. It's because we've never talked about the divorce."

"What do you want to know?"

"I want to understand why you broke up our family. What happened to you and Dad?"

"It goes way back," she says.

"Then start way back," I reply.

"We started in college."

"That part I know. Dad said you were majoring in finding a man."

"That's just like your father to say that. He's one to talk. Baseball star, bright future—he was the 'big man' on campus. I thought I was in love with him."

"You thought? What happened?"

"I had our future all mapped out. Baseball was such a long shot, but with his criminology degree, he had options like the FBI, CIA, or Secret Service. To this day, I still don't understand why he didn't set his sights on one of those agencies. But no, he had to settle for the state police as his career path. Do you know the potential he wasted? We could have lived in New York City or Washington, DC."

"He loved being a cop. He still does, and Pittsburgh is a great city."

"I hated being a cop's wife. It was so not me. Then when I had you, I was always worried that I would be a young widow raising a small child on my own."

"And you don't think that could have happened with the FBI or Secret Service?"

"If you keep up the comments, MJ, I won't tell you anymore."

"Got it."

"Your dad had these horrible work shifts that changed every two weeks. It made it difficult to make plans. Police work is twenty-four hours a day every day of the year. We were pretty much homebodies, and you know how much I love to travel. Then there were the emergencies where he had to report no matter what. It seemed like he was never home. Early in our marriage, I realized that this was not what I had signed up for."

"You never seemed unhappy."

"I got really good at hiding it. From the time you were small, I don't remember being happy, and I was always mad at your dad because of it. But I loved you, MJ. You were the reason I stayed in the marriage for so long. I wasn't about to mess up your life too."

As I open the door to the pub, the cozy atmosphere and tantalizing smells surround us. I realize that I am really hungry and could use a beer. With no delay, we are seated, and our drink orders are taken.

"So tell me why you and Dad don't talk."

"Your dad will never forgive me for divorcing him. Even though he wasn't happy either, he would have stayed in the marriage. Divorce equates failure to him, and you know how your dad hates to lose."

"I don't think you realize how much you hurt him."

"I think it was the settlement that hurt him. He was livid about the amount I received, and he was particularly upset that part of his retirement was affected. Once we signed the papers, he never talked to me again. I've never understood it. I earned the money. I stayed home and kept his house and raised you all those years. I have no regrets. I love my life now, and I've never looked back."

After the waitress takes our order, I lean back in the booth and gaze intently at the woman sitting across from me. I realize this is the first time I'm looking at her as a person and not just my mother.

"I know our relationship has suffered because of the divorce. I know how close you are with your dad. I want us to get our relationship back on track," she says.

"It's not that easy, Mom."

"Yes, it is. It's called forgiving and moving on."

"I guess it just takes longer for me . . . and Dad."

"I want you to remember, MJ, even knowing what I know now, I would marry your dad all over again just to have you in my life."

As I bite into my burger, I think about what she just said. Even though I have been angry with her since the divorce, I have never doubted her love for me. I wish I could say the same.

I am heading to class when the call comes.

"MJ, this is Sergeant Dean, your dad's commanding officer."

"I know you. My dad has mentioned you often."

"Are you in a situation where we can talk?" he asks.

"It's fine. I'm walking to class right now," I answer.

"Are you with friends?"

"No, it's just me."

"I had hoped you would be with someone."

"Why? What's this about?"

"I regret to inform you that there has been an explosion at our station house this morning. Most of the building is gone, and many of our troopers and office staff were critically and fatally injured." He pauses, giving me time to process what he just said. "I don't know how to tell you this, MJ, but your dad was thrown by the blast and died instantly. We are all in shock here. Your dad was one of my best officers and one of the finest men I know. I cannot tell you how sorry I am to give you this news."

I stop in my tracks. People continue to move around me as I stand there. I can't wrap my head around what Sergeant Dean just said. It can't possibly be true. I'm unable to put any words together to respond to him.

"Please let me know when you arrive. I can make arrangements for you, and I will help with whatever you need. I am so very sorry, MJ," he says as he ends the call.

I'm still standing in the same spot on the sidewalk with the phone to my ear. I feel like I've been hit with the same explosion that hit my dad. I turn and head back to my apartment. I feel like I'm going to be sick.

"Listen, MJ. You're distraught and in shock. I'm coming with you," Mom says.

"You're not coming with me, Mom!"

"Oh, but I am. You need me," she says without a doubt.

"Dad wouldn't want you there."

"I'm not going for your father. I'm going for you. You don't know what awaits you back there. I do, and I can make this easier for you."

"Easier! You think you can make this easier!" I find myself yelling at her.

"I didn't mean it that way. Within the last few years, I've buried my mother and father, so I know my way around these affairs. Do you want to plan your dad's funeral all by yourself?"

Hearing her say those words feels like a stab in my heart. I'm stunned. I wouldn't have a clue on how to begin to plan a funeral. Although I'm putting up a fight, deep down, I think I'm relieved to know that I won't be alone. Ending the call, I realize what Mom has been saying all along has come true.

"Someday, something bad is going to happen to your dad."

She was right for once. Sergeant Dean said this was some type of explosion. Was Dad trying to help other people? Did he have a seizure? I'm having trouble believing any of this is true. I can barely think straight as I throw some clothes in my luggage. It's a relief that Mom's making all the travel arrangements. This frees me up to arrange some time off from school. The trouble is that I have no idea how long I'll be gone.

I insisted that Mom book the first available flight. As I glance at my phone, I realize she'll be picking me up in about an hour. I told her not to include me in the hotel arrangements. I plan on staying at Dad's new home, and I made it perfectly clear that I want to stay there alone. She didn't raise a fuss. I guess she felt it was a battle not worth fighting.

I know I'll never be as close to my mother as I once was. I know this is my issue and not hers. As I grab my suit from the closet, I realize she's all I have left.

————————————————————————

Sitting in the pew, I feel like I'm in a horror movie or a nightmare that leaves me numb and exhausted. Jet lag has nothing to do with it. This gut-wrenching pain that I feel has taken on a life of its own. I feel like something is building up inside of me, and I'm going to explode if I don't let it out. I look at my clenched fists, and I realize

I want to punch something. I would welcome the physical pain any day over what I'm feeling now.

Life was going along as planned until I answered that call from Sergeant Dean. Everything has changed now. I'm going through the motions and doing what is expected of me, but I feel like nothing is real. I thought I was going to lose my dad once before, but everything worked out. Why couldn't that have happened this time? I feel like getting up from this pew, running out of the church, and leaving all this behind. Yet when I look at the casket, I feel my dad still near me, and I know that I will see this through to the end. I really want to talk to him one last time. I want to tell him what he's meant to me and how much I'm going to miss him in my life. He won't be there to see me graduate from med school or to meet my future wife or his first grandchild. I want so many things that will never happen now. I feel like I've lost my anchor, and I'm now free-floating. I can't see my life ever being the same. I can't see myself ever being the same.

Instead of following along with the prayers, my mind drifts back to the last few days. It's just like Dad to have all his affairs in order. I'm sure he wanted to make it easy for me. I guess his accident scared him enough that he preplanned his funeral and made sure his estate was in order. My mom thought that I would need her help in making all the arrangements. I think she was angry to find out that Dad had everything planned. It spoiled her desire to be needed. We argued about her staying. I was pretty sure Dad wouldn't have wanted her here, but I just didn't have the energy to fight her. She is sitting beside me now. It wasn't worth the effort to tell her no.

The last few days have blurred into each other. Flying out here, seeing Dad for the last time, staying at his new house, and talking with the funeral director, lawyer, minister, and the police filled up my days. It was a relief to know that all I had to do was show up and sign the papers. To my knowledge, Dad hadn't been practicing a religion since the divorce and accident. So it was a surprise to me that his plans requested a memorial service at the small church in his new neighborhood. Burial would be in the church's cemetery right outside town. Everyone was kind and extremely helpful in following his plans. They knew Dad's wishes, and they honored them.

My dad really didn't have any family but me, so I had no idea what to expect at the memorial service. To my surprise and to my dad's credit, the small church was packed. My dad's service is the first of three funerals that many of these people will attend over the next few days. The outpouring of sympathy and support that I have received has been overwhelming. Dad was well-loved and respected, and so many others share my loss.

His fellow officers have played a big part in his memorial service. Six of them carried his casket into the church and are standing watch over it now. Earlier in the service, Greg Dobler and Sergeant Dean spoke eloquently about Dad. I have to remember to thank them for doing this. I could never have done it, and I'm sure it wasn't easy for them either. Hopefully, they will give me a copy of their eulogies. I want to remember everything they said about him. Two troopers just sang a duet of "On Eagle's Wings." That was a part of his plans, and I remember it as one of his favorite hymns. Hearing the beautiful lyrics, I have no doubt that my dad is soaring with the eagles and in God's hands.

The last blessings have now been said, and I can't take my eyes off the casket as we exit the church. It is hard to believe my dad is in there and not here beside me. Mom and I are directed to the first limo, and the procession to the cemetery begins.

"MJ, that was a very beautiful and moving service. Don't you think?" my mom says after we are settled in the limo.

I shake my head and cut her off with a look. She gets the message, and we ride the rest of the way in silence.

At the entrance to the cemetery, there are two fire trucks parked on both sides of the lane.

Their ladders are raised, and there is a huge American flag stretched between the two rungs. As the hearse drives between the two trucks, firefighters and other people salute the casket as it passes by. Barely holding back my emotions, I think about how my dad would have been humbled by the respect and honor being shown.

I can see the tent set up in the distance as we enter the cemetery. "Just a little while longer," I say to myself.

Our funeral procession continues up the windy lane to the gravesite. When the limo comes to a stop, my mom and I walk together to the tent where the casket is in place over the grave. The site is situated near the woods. Alongside the tent, there is a large tree with branches weeping towards the ground. This seems to be appropriate to me, and I wonder if my dad picked this spot because of it.

My mom and I sit down in the front chairs facing the casket and wait for the other mourners to fill in behind us. I watch as a lady turns away from the group and walks right up to the casket. I didn't notice her before, and I wonder who she is and what she's doing. Then I see that she has a dog beside her. With a gasp, I realize it's Jed. How could I have forgotten about him? I have been so distracted by the events of the last few days that he didn't even enter my mind. This woman must be Haley, the lady my dad loved.

She helps Jed stand on his back legs and put his front paws on the flag-draped casket. He lifts his head to the sky and sniffs the air. He has a cast on his front leg and has a lot of his hair shaved. I realize it must be a result of the explosion. He whimpers as she helps him back to a standing position. She gives him a hand signal before she turns around and looks straight at me. Our eyes meet in a silent introduction. I can see she has been crying, and her grief mirrors my own. I feel an immediate and strong connection to her. She lowers her eyes first and walks to the back of the tent, where she joins two other mourners. I realize from the emblems on their clothing that they are from the Homeland Service Dog Association. The sight of them grabs at me. They came a long way to honor my dad.

I turn back around and gaze at Jed, lying there beside Dad's casket. The minister has started his last prayers by now, but I don't hear them. All my attention is on Jed, the dog that changed my dad's life. I watch him lift his head as the honor guard fires its three-volley gun salute to their fallen comrade. As the officers fold up the flag, I can hear a lone bugler playing "Taps" off in the distance. I see Jed struggle and whimper as he makes his way up to a sitting position. His ears lift to the mournful sound of the trumpet as he sits alert and alone by his partner's casket. I hear him whimper again, and I become aware of people crying around me. I lower my head and join them.

When the honor guard presents me with the flag, I clutch it tightly to my chest as if some of my dad could seep deep inside me. The graveside prayers are now concluded. The funeral director hands me a rose and directs me to put it on the casket and say my last goodbyes. I don't have any words for this. Saying goodbye to my dad will take me the rest of my life.

"MJ, you have to lead this now," my mother whispers to me.

I somehow manage to do what's expected of me. I stand and look at the flower and then gently lay it on the center of the casket. Mine is the first rose. After I do this, I walk over to Jed and go down on my knees before him. I whisper to him as I give him a gentle hug. "You changed his life, you know. Dad loved you, and I know you loved him." Jed looks up at me with his big brown eyes, and I feel his loss too.

I get up and follow my mom and the funeral director outside of the tent. People are gathering and talking all around me, but I can't seem to concentrate on any of them because I'm looking for Haley. A woman approaches me, blocking my view and interrupting my search.

"MJ, I was so afraid that I wouldn't get to talk to you. We haven't met, but I'm Alexandra Jennings, your Dad's neighbor."

"Oh yes. He's mentioned you," I reply.

"We were becoming close, and I'm just so shocked and devastated by all this. My son, Brandon, is inconsolable. If I can be of help in any way, please let me know. I'm a realtor if you need help with the house." She gives me a hug, which I barely return and is cut short by my mom.

"Thank you for your condolences. MJ appreciates all your support. The funeral director is directing us to leave now," she says. Before I can even get a word out, my mom takes hold of my arm and directs me away from the woman and the gravesite.

After walking a few steps, I remember that I didn't get to talk to Haley. As I turn and look back toward the departing mourners, I see her getting in a car with Jed. I try to yell her name, but she's too far away to hear me. My mom is saying something to the funeral director, and they are both ushering me into the limo. I balk at leaving the gravesite and turn around to go back. I'm not ready to leave my dad yet, and I want to talk to Haley. My mom grabs my arm and turns me back to the limo.

"If you don't leave, MJ, the others won't either. It's over. The grave diggers are waiting to do their job now," Mom says as she slides into the backseat.

With a final look back, I follow her into the limo. She puts her arms around me, and I realize it feels good to be held. This has been the worst day of my life.

CHAPTER 38

HALEY DUNCAN

It has been four days since I arrived home from the funeral. I'm having a really hard time accepting that Mark's gone. I'm not alone in this. Jed's not the same dog. Even though he is getting physically stronger every day, he is lethargic and unresponsive at times. Noises that never bothered him before startle him now. There are times when he seems skittish and fearful. I know some of these reactions are due to the explosion, but I also know some are because he misses Mark. Dogs mourn. I have seen it in my own dogs, and I see it in Jed now. I can feel his grief.

Magic and Thunder sense a difference in Jed too. They are watchful of him and stay close by. They encourage but don't gang up on him when he shows no interest in playing or engaging in their wrestling matches. When I got up in the middle of the night yesterday, I found my two dogs sleeping like bookends beside Jed. I don't know what motivated them to do this, but their actions touched my heart. Animals, like people, need support getting through hard times. I took my pillow off the bed and joined them on the floor. Their gentle breathing lulled me back to sleep.

Jed's mourning for Mark compounds my own sadness. I've been down this road before, and I know that time will numb the pain of loss. As excruciating as it hurts right now, I know that eventually I'll be able to move on. But I won't be the same. Every tragedy changes who we are and how we look at life.

It's been over a week since I've been at school. I'm sure my students are wondering what happened to me. Tomorrow I will return to my classroom, and my life will return to its normal patterns. My heart is a different story. It needs to forge another detour around this new heartache.

As I am getting the dogs ready for their daily walk, I hear a knock at my door. It takes us all by surprise. Magic and Thunder rush to the door, barking wildly, while Jed hangs back by my side. Much to their dismay, I put them all in a down/stay before I open the door.

"MJ!" I exclaim, surprised.

"Hi. I was afraid you wouldn't know me. We never officially met," he replies.

"Even if I hadn't seen you at the funeral, I would still know you. You're the image of your father."

"That is the nicest thing I've heard all week," he says.

Looking closely at him, I can see the wear and tear of the last days showing on his face. "Come in," I add quickly. "Say hello to Jed and meet Magic and Thunder." I release the dogs from their down/stay, and the three surround him. "Thunder is the bigger of the two."

MJ goes down to their level, offering pets and belly rubs, but he focuses most of his attention on Jed, petting and talking to him softly. I remain silent, giving them time together. I find it bittersweet to watch his interaction with Jed. It reminds me so much of Mark. After some time, MJ stands up and looks at me.

"Please take a seat. Can I get you anything to eat or drink? You've come a long way," I ask.

"No thanks," he says as he takes a seat on the sofa. "I changed my flight so I could leave out of your regional airport. I needed to see you. I wanted to finally meet you in person."

"I'm so glad you came."

"Dad wasn't a big talker, but he told me you were special. He said that you were the best thing that ever happened to him." With a sad smile, he adds, "He loved you, you know."

"I know he did."

"Dad was despondent when you left. He thought he blew it with you. You know, my parents never let me see the bitterness of their divorce. I was in my first year of college back then, and I wasn't very perceptive. I thought life just centered around me."

I study his face as he pauses. Even his voice sounds like Mark's.

"Looking back, I can see that my mom moved on easily to a brand-new life. But it left my dad with deep scars, and he struggled for a long time. After the divorce, he didn't have much good to say about marriage or women. Then he met you, and it was the happiest I've ever seen him."

I see him shake his head and struggle to continue. I remain silent, allowing him time.

"He knew your leaving was all his fault, and he told me he was going to make it right. I thought he had until I found this at the house addressed to you." He opens his backpack as he continues. "It was sitting on the mantle by that great painting you had made for him. I could have mailed it, but I think Dad would have liked the idea of me delivering it personally to you."

He hands me an envelope with a small box attached. "I'll let you open it when you're alone. I know all about it. Dad told me in one of our last conversations."

He glances at his watch, which I recognize as Mark's. He would be happy to know that MJ is wearing it now. "My plane leaves in a couple of hours, so I really can't stay much longer. I'm sorry I didn't meet you at the funeral. I feel awful about that."

"It's OK. I understand. Funerals are hard. I really appreciate your coming all the way out here. You don't know how much this means to me."

"I have to be going. Do you think it would be OK if I give you a hug?" MJ asks sheepishly.

"I would like that."

As I embrace this handsome young man, it almost feels like Mark's arms around me again. I hug him back fiercely, memorizing his feel. As we break apart, I gently say to him. "Go and make a difference with your life. Your dad was so proud of you. Keep him with you always."

"I will," he says.

He turns to Jed, cradles his head in his hands, and says something quietly to him that I can't hear. Looking over at me, he asks, "Will Jed live with you now? I know that is what my dad wanted."

"I'm not sure. Your dad received ownership of Jed with the placement. If Jed recovers fully, the Service Dog Association will help me decide what is best for him."

He thought about this for a moment and said, "Maybe there is another life out there that Jed can change."

"Maybe," I answer.

"Would it be OK if I contacted you from time to time? I think Dad would like us to keep in touch."

"That would mean a lot to me," I answer.

"Bye," he says with a slight wave.

"Thank you, MJ. Be safe."

I am filled with emotion as I watch him stride down the walk. When he reaches the car, I notice him stop and get something from the back. He lifts out the painting I had made for Mark and turns and walks back to me.

"I almost forgot. When I went through Dad's personal belongings, I didn't feel right keeping this. I think he would want you to have it."

Tears spring to my eyes as I gaze at the painting. "Thank you. I will cherish it," I say.

"I know my dad did," he replies.

"But I'll only keep it for the time being. Some day when you have your own home, it should honor your mantle like it did your dad's. It will be here waiting for you until that time comes."

With a silent nod and a hint of a smile, MJ turns and walks back to the rental car. He pauses to look back at me. He gives me a slight wave, and then he is gone.

I slowly enter the house and cross to the fireplace. I place the picture on my mantle just like Mark had it on his. Sitting down, I look closely at the envelope and box sitting on my coffee table. "My last gift from Mark," I say to myself. I carefully open the envelope. There is only one sheet of paper, and it is in Mark's handwriting.

> *Dear Haley,*
>
> *You were right to give us time. I needed it to think clearly and put everything in perspective. I want you to know that I was utterly and totally wrong. Saying that I would never marry again was a defense I built up over time to cope with my failed marriage. I got so used to saying it that it just became second nature to me. I had been saying it for so long that I actually believed it. Then, I met you.*
>
> *I never thought I would meet someone like you. I never thought someone like you could love someone like me. Committing to you was never a problem for me. I did that the first week I met you. I have always been sure about us. I just had trouble leaving my past behind me. But that is exactly where it belongs—behind me—and that's where it is going to stay. I want you with me always. I can't imagine my life without you.*
>
> *Here is where I want you to put this letter down because I have a question to ask you . . .*

The letter stops there. I know what he was going to ask me. I gently remove the wrapping from the small box. I recognize the labeling as the same jeweler who crafted my bracelet and necklace. Whatever is inside, Mark had it designed especially for me. As I open the small box, I find an exquisite ring resting on a bed of satin. I catch my breath as I look closely at it. There are two aquamarine stones intertwined in gold and surrounded by clusters of diamonds. Mark chose our shared birthstone for the center of the ring. I remember how we laughed the day we discovered that our birthdays were only days apart. I slip the ring slowly on my finger. The diamonds sparkle, and the two light-blue stones are crafted so that they almost look as one. Crying, I whisper the words, "I take thee, Mark. . . ."

EPILOGUE

Today is the one-year anniversary of Mark's death. It is evening, and I am sitting outside watching the dogs play. In the weeks following the explosion, the investigation found that the bomb was a retaliatory strike for a huge arms bust the station orchestrated. Major kingpins were indicted and are still awaiting trial. I didn't follow the story. It didn't matter to me.

Jed continues to limp, although it certainly doesn't slow him down any. After the accident, it took time for him to heal physically and mentally. After a number of months, I had him re-evaluated by the trainers at the Homeland Service Dog Association. Although I officially own him now, I did not want to stop him from the job he was raised to do. The trainers agreed that Jed should stay with me, but they asked if I would be willing to go through the training to be an ambassador for their program. Jed could act as my demonstration dog. This ended up being the best thing that could have happened to Jed and me.

Since then, we have made frequent presentations to church groups, schools, hospitals, and corporations. Not only are we spreading information about the life-changing work these service dogs do, but Jed and I are fundraising as well. Last month, we made a very successful presentation to a roomful of lawyers at their regional convention. Not only did Homeland receive many pledges of donations, but I received a dinner invitation from their chairman, a real dog lover. We've gone out a few times so far, and it's been fun. He is thoughtful and kind and adores my dogs.

To my delight, MJ has stayed in close contact. He continues to struggle with Mark's death, but in me, he's found a sounding board for his grief. I sense Mark's strength in him, and I know that he won't let this tragedy define him. He is very much his father's son. Having MJ in my life feels like Mark's ongoing gift to me. For this, I am extremely thankful. He adds a dimension to my life that I never had before. I feel we will always be connected by the loss we share.

Last spring, I made my final trip to Pittsburgh. After many delays, Mark's gravestone was finally finished and set in place. MJ couldn't make the trip and asked me to go in his place. He needed assurance that his wishes were carried out and that the stone was a fitting memorial to his dad. I took Jed with me to the cemetery. To my surprise, etched into the stone were Mark and Jed walking into the distance, just like in the painting. Life came full circle for me that day.

Magic, Thunder, and Jed only know how to live in the moment. This is something they remind me to do every day. As I watch them frolic and play, I realize what a beautiful night it is. There is a slight breeze blowing and a bit of a chill in the air. Every once in a while, I see the dogs lift their heads to the sky and smell the wind. It seems as if something or someone is speaking to them. I would like to believe it is Jack and Mark checking in on their dogs and maybe checking in on me too. I feel lucky and blessed to have been loved by two wonderful men. They are never far from me. I have learned that the heart has the ability to heal again and again, and it has the capacity to love over and over.

On this anniversary, I think back on my life and the journey it has been. I will not let the tragedies of my life become roadblocks for me. Every detour I've encountered not only changed my journey but also changed me. As I watch Jed, his black coat blending into the darkness, his head lifted to the night sky, I realize my story is far from over, and neither is his.

END

ABOUT THE AUTHOR

Carol Fricke is a retired teacher and coach from Derry Township School District in Hershey, Pennsylvania. She grew up in Fryburg, a small town. After high school, she attended Indiana University of Pennsylvania where she competed on their gymnastics team. Following graduation, she moved to Hershey where she spent the next thirty-five years teaching Health and Physical Education at Hershey High School and coaching gymnastics for thirty of those years.

Being an animal lover her entire life, Carol knew her retirement had to involve her passion for dogs. She started volunteering with the Susquehanna Service Dogs in Grantville, Pennsylvania after reading about the organization in a local paper. The trainers, volunteers, puppy raisers and dogs that she met there inspired her to write.

Carol shares her life with her husband, a daughter, a granddaughter, and two Newfoundland dogs. She spends her time playing music, tennis, and as vice-chair for the South Hanover Township Parks & Recreation Board.

For more information, visit **www.CarolFricke.com**

Acknowledgments

A big thank you to Jacquelin Cangro, my first editor, for her guidance and expertise.

Another big thank you to Patricia Ploss, my publisher from Centaur Books, for giving me a chance to make my dream come true.

Printed in the USA
CPSIA information can be obtained
at www.ICGtesting.com
LVHW041945021123
762269LV00014B/11/J